PECK'S SALUTE

By Tim Mahoney

Also by Tim Mahoney

Shipwreck Bay

Year of the Rooster

Reverse Lightning

The Resurrection of John Dillinger

Dead Messenger

Dead Like Lazarus

Dead a Long Time

If the Dead Could Speak

Secret Partners

We're Not Here

Hollaran's World War

First edition

*Copyright Tim Mahoney
2019*

*Cover art by Randall Roden
rodencreative.com*

Cover photos:

Background, the author

Foreground, courtesy Thanh Nguyen

ISBN: 978-0-9908974-8-4

I says to myself,
there ain't no telling
but I might come to be
a murderer myself, yet,
and then how would I like it?

Huckleberry Finn

Love means never having to say you're sorry.

From the movie *Love Story*

Dedicated to my brothers in arms,

D-4-2 First Aviation Brigade

"Ground-pounders of the Delta."

CHAPTER ONE

Before I go to prison for assaulting that nun, I'd like to say: ~~The bitch deserved it.~~

I'm truly remorseful, Your Honor.

The trouble began in the Year of Our Lord 1966.

I wore patent leather shoes and gray trousers with dark military stripes running down the leg.

My gray schoolboy blazer announced to every Hell-bound Protestant that I adhered to the One True Faith at Saint Sebastian High School.

However, I spurned Salvation, so for the Nth time, I sat in the Bad Boy chair in Sister Charles' office.

My father squirmed in the Angry Parent chair across from me.

Sister Charles! Dominatrix of the Jersey Inquisition.

Said torments took place in the office behind the cloak room.

I have no idea why it was called the cloak room, since Saint Sebastian students never wore cloaks.

Just another example, Your Honor, of the unreasonable nature of Authority.

Anyway, my crime was cutting Latin class, hiding in the hedges, smoking cigarettes and mocking Authority.

"Smoking?" Barked my father, a pack a day smoker himself.

He leaped out of that hard wood chair and slapped my face.

"Well!" said Sister Charles, "I certainly didn't expect that."

She sat back with a glowing smile.

She happy-fingered her rosary beads.

Do I need to point out, Your Honor, that she enjoyed it?

And so did he.

Oh, yes, John Adams Peckfogle, "concerned parent," put on a wonderful act for the nuns.

I ultimately became a US-Army-Certified Professional Writer.

I might have been a star student in English composition.

But obviously, I failed the lesson on paragraphing.

A paragraph is a self-contained discourse formed into a single, unifying idea.

I know that, Sister.

But I am compelled to disobey you, Sister Charles, by my inner voice.

I was perfectly content to write in formal paragraphs until I discovered that it meant so much to you.

Now I write in a style disjointed you could say sometimes omitting proper, punctuation just because it pisses you off.

I'm talking to you, Sister Charles, you who hanged me by my tie for the crime of writing one sentence at a time.

I know I taunted you, Sister, and provoked your sweet loving nature until you were compelled to resort to corporal punishment.

I made you do it.

Because I am the Devil.

You rushing down the aisle, rosary beads clacking against your hidden thigh.

You, named for Charles Borromeo, Bishop of Milan, cousin of Pope Somebody the Third.

Charles Borromeo, a murdering Medici.

Your hero, "Saint" Charles, who burned women alive.

And now your scrubbed-clean hands grab my tie.

And lift me out of my chair.

And march me down to the principal's office to sign me up for another week of detention.

Don't you know, Sister, that I adore detention?

I'll tell you what I've learned in the years since you collared me, Sister Charles.

We're all as guilty as sin.

Every one of us has stood there, gaping oafs, as our opportunities to do the right thing slipped by.

This is our greatest crime.

The Sin of Omission, as they say in the Church.

You know exactly what I'm talking about, don't you, Sister?

I've seen you on your knees in the chapel, begging forgiveness from Our Savior.

Detention was run by Miss Malecki.

Her face launched a thousand sessions of student masturbation, even though her body was tight-wrapped in bargain-store cloth.

A curly-haired Polish blonde, pale of face, kind, and with beautiful blue eyes, Miss Malecki was apprenticing under the stern auspices of the One, Holy and Apostolic.

She wore skirts practically down to her ankles.

She favored purple blouses, the color of Lent and atonement.

"Miss Malecki, can I go to the bathroom?"

Says I, grubby little hand raised high above my one-piece desk.

"Certainly, John Jay," she said.

She gave me that conspiracy smile.

"Don't dawdle."

Which meant she'd give me time to smoke a cigarette.

Love is patient, love is kind, love is Miss Malecki.

The boys room was clear of its usual stinky and threatening occupants, aka my buddies.

My friends were probably at Mombo Bill's already, sucking down Rheingolds in the company of Staten Island tugboat crews.

My enemies, the Collegiates, who kissed up to the nuns, they were all home, studying algebra and paragraphs.

A thick wire screen over the window was the only thing between me and the free world.

I didn't realize I'd soon be looking through a similar screen meant to deflect hand grenades.

I was the embodiment of my favorite Latin word, *Ignoramus.*

Which means: We do not know.

As I blew cigarette smoke through that screen, I calculated my chances with Miss Malecki, and when I returned to the detention home room, it was just me and my love.

I was the only boy on double detention that day.

I stunk of Camels and the boys room.

Miss Malecki, correcting essays, stunk of Chanel No. 5

She held a No.2 pencil in her hand.

And was No. 1 in my heart.

Her thick eyeglasses only made her sexier.

"Miss Malecki," I said, "what year did you graduate?"

She looked up at me. "What a strange question, J.J."

Her curiosity turned into a shy smile.

"Graduate college," she asked, "is that what you mean?"

"Yes, Miss Malecki."

"May of last year," she said.

"Just thinking," I said.

"Thinking?"

I was 17, and she was 23.

In May, when I turned 18, we'd be legally free to consummate our mutual passion.

I set June as our wedding date.

I had already decided that we would abstain from sex on Sundays, because she'd definitely need a break from the workout I intended to give her.

When he learned of our marriage, my old man would be furious, but if he whipped me after my 18th birthday, then I could call the cops.

Or find the balls to kill him, either one.

His name is John Adams but he goes by Adam. You may have heard of him, "Adam" Peckfogle, animal rights crusader. And yes, he's a whip-wielding bully in private.

Yes, he hit his children with a whip, also called a crop or a stick, the kind carried by jockeys.

And that's why our family is scattered to the winds.

There'll be no Peckfogles at our wedding, I guarantee.

The nuptial crowd will include Miss Malecki's scandalized relatives, and my buddies from the Bayway gang.

We'll be married on motorcycles and then ride over the Goethals Bridge for a wild drunken reception at Mombo Bill's.

"J.J.?"

"Yes, Miss Malecki."

I loved when she used my nickname.

"Have you finished your assignment?"

"No, Miss Malecki."

"As soon as you're finished, we can both go home."

Her sweet boner-inducing voice!

So I sat down and finished writing: I WILL NOT BE DISRUPTIVE IN CLASS.

I'd been instructed to write this 100 times, each on a single line in a marble composition book.

And this is where I learned the virtues of the very short paragraph.

In detention.

"Miss Malecki?"

"Yes?"

"Is 88 times enough?"

She smiled. "Sure."

Many Catholics reserve their adoration for the Virgin Mary, but it's you I adore, Miss Malecki.

The Blessed Virgin of Bayway.

I'd put a statue of you on every lawn in New Jersey.

"Private Peckfogle."

"Sir?"

"Are you religious?"

"I hate religion, sir, it is the opiate of the asses."

"Well, somebody's praying for you."

I shuffled my combat boots on the wooden floor of company HQ.

"The Judge Advocate has deferred your case."

Captain Clark sat back in his chair and glowed. "He considers you a worm, Peckfogle, not worth prosecuting – did I say worm? Make that maggot."

"Is that all sir?"

"No, that is not all, Peckfogle. There is an Alpha Romeo Tango One Five coming at you, so report back here at Oh Nine Hundred tomorrow."

"I can't be reduced in rank, sir, I'm already at the bottom."

"Forfeiture of 30 days pay and count yourself lucky that we don't have KP over here."

I saluted with my bandaged hand.

"Don't bother showing up on payday."

"Got it, sir."

Despite his gruff talk, Captain Clark likes me.

I do a distasteful job for him and very likely he lobbied to reduce the Courts Martial to a simple Article-15.

"That is all, Peckfogle."

I walked out into the sweaty dust, a guy in a war zone, carrying no weapons at all.

The United States of America, land of the free and home of the draft dodger, had sent me over to this Very Important Country to kill its residents, who were of no importance whatsoever, which is why they were slaughtered wholesale.

For the crime of being Not Important to America.

Being a Paid Professional Killer was an assignment I did not find intellectually fulfilling.

There are only two people I'd like to kill: Sister Charles Borromeo, and my father, John Adams Peckfogle.

And neither of them are available right now.

Number of Vietnamese civilians who have assaulted me? Zero.

Therefore I wish to kill zero Vietnamese civilians.

I've been pretty good at that so far.

I've found the Vietnamese to be a decent bunch, especially considering that we're stomping around their country, killing them by the thousands.

And there's one Vietnamese I like in particular.

Of course she's a "girl."

And a Catholic.

And much older than me.

She's kind of like Miss Malecki, but with dark eyes and bad acne.

I like the older woman.

They expect less, and with me, they get it.

No, my girlfriend is a not a whore, like you're probably thinking.

She is a bookkeeper.

I passed the Main Gate, where the MPs know me well, and appreciate my generosity, and I gave a mock salute to the gatehouse, and those bastards laughed and said, Peckfogle where's your pass, and I said Private Last Class Peckfogle, he don't need no pass, does he bubba?

You've got to talk in ignorant hillbilly tones when you converse with the MPs.

This I leaned during my incarceration at LBJ.

I slipped onto the carriage behind a cyclo, and sat underneath the scant canvas shade of its tattered top.

I needed to give no instructions to the driver, my friend Du Ky. I just sat back sweaty, sucking in the oily wind, and watching as the beautiful fucked up tropical countryside flew by.

Me a sweaty knight in faded fatigues.

Du Ky my page, his Honda my horse.

Sir Peckfogle, on the road to Cong Ly Street, where danger and riches lurked in equal proportion.

Here's Cong Ly Street: Narrow, muddy, lined with moldy stone buildings two or three stories tall, in front of which squat mama-sans in conical hats selling candy, dead fish, mangoes, tarot card readings, orange soda, vegetables with dirty roots, lichi nuts, mountain apples and squawking chickens, all peddled from under sun-blasted umbrellas, and the whole street choking on exhaust from buzzing motor scooters, and swarming with child beggars and shoeshine boys.

It's hot.

There has never been a cool day in the entire history of South Vietnam. This is a country where you can get sunburned in the rain.

My rented quarters stand one magnificent story above the sign STEAM BATH MASSAGE, next to the cockroach-ridden movie theater showing LOVE STORY with RYAN O'NEAL.

Du Ky let me off at the STEAM BATH MASSAGE, griping because the movie theater hadn't shown a new film in months.

"Where's Butch Cassidy?" he asked. "Never come here. I must go into Saigon, I suppose."

"Yes, take a day off," I said.

"Days off, I don't have."

I paid him $2, American.

That's another thing we've done to these people, converted them to dollars and the harsh English language.

Their language is sing-song and nasal. Ours is full of hisses, like the warning of a snake.

Once you accept payment in dollars and hiss in English, the United States of America owns you.

When I burst through the door, my love, ~~Miss Malecki~~ Merci, looked up from her adding machine and snarled: "Slow day!"

I walked around the sagging plywood counter, gathered her short fragrant hair in a bunch, and kissed her ugly face.

"Ow," she said.

"I love you," I said.

"No way!" She pushed me away with one hand, the red nails of the other clacking on the adding machine. "Too hot," she said.

"It's like a steam bath in here," I said.

Same joke every day.

"How is your hand?" she asked.

"Healing," I said, and held up the bandaged edge for inspection.

"Waste of money," she said.

She was talking about my tattoo.

She turned that roundish scowling, scarred face to me, red lipstick, whorish eye-shadow, angry eyes.

She was not really Vietnamese but Cambodian-Corsican, product of a refugee mother and a dark-skinned scoundrel from the French Foreign Legion.

Cambodians have not exactly been welcome in Vietnam, given the long and tortured history between them.

Also, it's an unfortunate fact of local culture that light-skinned people are much preferred, as are those whose ancestry is unmixed with Foreign Legionnaires.

So Merci hasn't had the easiest life.

Rejection, nuns, and the Latin Mass, it's what we have in common.

She yanked paper tape out of the adding machine, handed it to me and said, "Shit-faced cheapskates," and lit a Basto in her lipsticked lips, using a lighter stolen out of the pockets of some drunken Marine.

Cigarette dangling from chapped lips, she peeked out the door, looking for Crocodile.

From inside the steam room, some lonely GI moaned with $10 worth of pleasure.

It's all a passing show, dude, I muttered, and a $10 hand job is only going to lighten your wallet.

"How much you short?" I asked Merci.

"You kidding?" she said, "All fifty five."

"They docked my pay," I said.

"Fuck a bunch of assholes," said Merci.

"My sentiments exactly."

"They eat shit."

There's a very particular kind of English you learn when your teachers are GIs.

The coprofagia Merci referred to was practiced by the Cong Ly Street Association, and it's a complex situation that can't be tossed off in just a sentence. The "street association" is a franchise granted by the Binh Xuyen gang, which makes the American Mafia look like choir boys. There can be no civic justice in Saigon, because the Binh Xueyn are the gangsters, and have infiltrated the police. They're also dope runners and spies for the VC and for a dozen factional militias. In our neighborhood, their chief thug was a grinning pervert named Crocodile.

"Leave it to me," I said.

She closed the door, keeping out the street noise. Down the interior plywood hallway stumbled a drunken GI, maybe nineteen years old, buckling his belt over a hard-on that had been reduced by Sanny's delicate hands in return for a sweaty $10 bill.

He was too drunk to notice us.

"Come back *min oy,*" Merci called to him.

If a local says *"min oy"* to another local, it means "sweetheart."

If she says it to a GI it means: "See you next payday."

When the door shut and Boner Boy was out on the street, Merci said: "Bad time of the month."

She wasn't talking about her menstrual cycle, but those five days before Long Binh payday, when everybody was broke.

"I'll talk to Crocodile," I said.

"Good, maybe he listens to you," said Merci, and blew smoke.

Cough cough.

"In the next life ..." she said.

"Yes?"

"In the next life I want to live where it snows and people wear fur hats."

"Alaska," I said.

"Beautiful snow," she said. "I have not seen such things."

I walked out to the street, and one shop over to the Marilyn Monroe.

These are my neighbors: The movie theater that's been showing Love Story for six months, and the Marilyn Monroe café, serving iced coffee, hot rumors, and warm bottles of "33" since this War began.

A poster of Marilyn nailed above the awning showed her with wide-mouth smile, wild blond hair, and an oceanic swell of breasts.

There are whole blocks on this street that cater to American charity staffers, spies, construction workers, deserters, diplomats, journalists and war tourists, and these neighborhoods aren't really Vietnam anymore.

And don't get me started on Long Binh, which is a suburb of Sacramento, complete with chlorine-stinky swimming pools, casinos and nightclub acts. I expect Sammy Davis Junior to show up at the Foxhole Lounge any day now.

Crocodile was parked in his usual spot, a dark alley between the Marilyn Monroe and a gold ~~smuggler~~ merchant who plied his trade from behind iron bars, with the added protection of a hard-faced goon at the door.

One of Crocodile's silent female goons.

I don't know where he found these women, but they all seemed as if they'd lost their souls in a torture chamber.

And maybe they had.

Croc himself sat on his yellow Honda. He was a Cyclops, with one eye gone. He had lost his binocular vision and wasn't the knife fighter of old.

He was about forty years old, quite an accomplishment to live that long, given his profession, location, and his preference for knives over firearms.

He wore US Army fatigues and a boonie hat.

That one bad eye was a veiny white.

He focused the other on me.

He was a tough, wiry little bastard , and his teeth gleamed gold.

"Speck Focal," he said, deliberately twisting my name.

Oh yeah, the bastard could speak English better than half these hillbilly GIs. He loved to twist names and words into his own private meanings, snarling in French, English and the local lingo.

"Speck Focal, why do you stand in front of me where I cannot see my street? Please tell me Speck Focal, because I would love to understand you worthless Americans just once before I die."

"I need fifty five dollars worth of love," I said.

"Is that all?"

"Or maybe you could call it mercy."

"Mercy," Crocodile said, and grinned in gold. "That is a very good word," he said, "a French word I believe that translates to *chao em* in the language of our divided and tragic land."

Then he spit at the street and said: "Where's my 55?"

Crocodile liked the number 55, for some mysterious reason.

He also liked Oscar Mayer hot dogs cut up, laid over cold rice and sprinkled with *nuoc mam*, but then, to each his own.

The monthly price of his extortion might just as well have been $50 or $75, but $55 in greenbacks had been his price ever since he'd fatally stabbed Gee Nan, his predecessor in the Cong Ly Protection Association.

In the throat.

Gee Nan died on this sidewalk, feral dogs licking his blood.

"You know what happens next, don't you, Speck Focal?"

"No mercy?" I said, "what about credit?"

"An American concept," he said, "which requires trust."

He wagged a stubby finger at me. "Sadly lacking in these unfortunate times."

I said: "No money coming in this payday."

"The whole base? Can it be? America is running out of dollars?"

"No, just me. How about I pay double next month?"

Crocodile spun the accelerator on his Honda, making a racket that echoed down the dark moldy alley.

I was suddenly aware that it was a hundred degrees.

I unbuttoned my fatigue shirt and fanned myself with its flaps.

"You cannot understand, today is the only day" he said. "America has a future, but in Vietnam there is only yesterday and now."

He cleared his throat of cigarette phlegm, and then lapsed into pidgin, just to mock me.

"Pay later, no good, GI, same-same never."

"You know what it says on our currency?" I asked. Getting a cold stare in return, I supplied the answer: "In God We Trust."

"So when you become a God, I will trust you."

"She's had a hard life, Crocodile, she's been paying and paying."

He spat in the street and said: "Perhaps you are the partner I've been seeking, Peckfogle, I've long considered you a clever and capable fellow ..."

Now that he wanted something from me, he pronounced my name correctly.

"... you are the one, perhaps, who can sneak a duffel bag through the Heavenly Gate. You know there has been a problem of late, which I believe your scholars call the Protestant Ethic."

"The what?"

"You know, thou shalt not."

"I am not a drug smuggler, Crocodile, those guys go to prison for 40 years."

"How much is 55 cartons worth inside the gate?"

"Let's see," I said, "200 cigarettes per carton... "

"Think of the fortune we can split, Jack Jay."

Oh, so now it was Jack Jay.

Along Cong Ly Street, the average price for a Blend cigarette was $1. But on base, the price could be as high as $10, depending on how tightly Colonel Sadler had the gate sealed.

Crocodile lit a Kool.

Only the elite could afford to put a sweet-menthol Kool between their lips. Kools were the perfect refreshing cigarette for a 100-degree country, and the best foundation for making The Blend, and therefore rare and expensive.

A Kool's menthol disguised the bitter taste of cheap brown opium. That crap was the specialty of the Binh Xuyen, who had been running opium, and financing a huge gangster militia, since this nation was a French colony.

"Perhaps I can offer your lady," he said, cigarette bobbing in his golden mouth, "a lifetime pass, or as you might say, freedom from Street Tax."

Lifetime?

That could be about ten seconds in this country.

"So I buy from you a shitload of Blend sticks," I said, "and sell them on the base. To whom?"

"Oh, we have friends on base. But they are not liked by the MPs, as you are. They cannot pass Main Gate so easy. You have been observed passing without challenge through the gate, and it is said you know every MP by name."

"So I sell the shitload to your mystery buddies at..."

"$55,000 for the lot, wholesale."

So this batch was worth $11,000 on Cong Ly Street and $55,000 on the base.

Math genius that I am, I intuited a $44,000 profit.

"Only the thing I need," said Crocodile, "is a good faith payment of $11,000."

"Are you nuts?"

"Finance! Your whore has a calculator, yes?"

"Where do I get $11,000?"

"Okay, I will finance half. The manufacturer must be paid. Your half, $5500 to help with expenses. As you say in America, I am not made of the money that grows on trees."

"Okay, so let me get this straight: I give you $5500, smuggle in a duffel bag of Blend, deliver to your inside man and then ..."

"I will do the rest. I will collect, for sure. Then I repay your $5500, plus another $5500 for your trouble."

"So I take all the risk, finance half the deal and get ... "

"Be an optimist," Crocodile said. "You double your money in one day, and do a big favor for your beloved whore and her business."

"And Sanny too," I bargained. "And all Mister Tin's property, including the Marilyn Monroe café. All freed from Street Tax after the deal."

"The whore and her steam bath only," Crocodile insisted. He stuck out his grotesque, leprous hand. "Let's make the deal."

I shuddered and shook on it.

I shouldn't have done it, Your Honor.

I know that now.

Crocodile checked his gold watch. It was a ladies' watch, ripped from the arm of a UN attaché.

"Sundown," he said, "April 26th, I will see you in the *Café des Prostituées*, and we will plan how to make our fortune."

CHAPTER TWO

In southern Vietnam, April is the cruelest month. The monsoons begin in May, and the constant rains, while by no means cool, bring the heat down a half a degree below vicious.

But in April, it can be 95 degrees with sweat-lodge humidity, even at three in the morning. Peckfogle's only defense against this all-night swelter was one greasy, black, pitiful rotating Westinghouse fan.

That fan blew hot air on the skinny, sleepless form of Peckfogle, naked but for blue jean cutoffs. He squirmed atop an Army sleeping bag. The bag was spread on a floor of green-and-white tiles. On the other side of a white-painted steel kitchen table, Merci slept on a grimy double bed. She was short, thick, had long black hair, and wore a sleeveless olive-drab t-shirt many sizes too large for her.

Peckfogle could not sleep beside her, it was much too hot for that. Merci gave off heat like a stove. The floor was cooler, and offered the only chance for slumber.

Peckfogle could never quite understand what women needed. He'd disappointed every woman he'd ever known, starting with his mother, his sister and every Saint Sebastian nun. Only Miss Malecki loomed soft and beautiful in his dreams.

Miss Malecki, oh Miss Malecki.

In his latest Miss Malecki dream, he was boning her in the cloak room while Sister Charles, ruler in hand, whipped herself to Holy Orgasm.

All it took to puncture that dream was a mosquito. Peckfogle awoke, swatted and cried: "Leave me alone!"

He glanced through the picket of table legs and saw Merci was dead asleep. He angled the fan under the table to get a better share of the artificial breeze that kept mosquitoes away. Merci, asleep, was about as mobile as a sack of cement. She never seemed to flinch, turn, twitch or snore. He envied her. Peckfogle hadn't had a decent night's sleep since he'd been inducted.

It was rare for such a low-ranked GI to have off-base privileges. Although, in Peckfogle's case, these privileges were informally granted. This was lucky for Merci, because Peckfogle's presence had probably saved her life.

A woman was better off with a protector, preferably American, in this neighborhood. Peckfogle took that responsibility seriously, but it didn't seem fair that Merci slept soundly while he worried all night.

From the kitchen table Peckfogle gripped a Zippo lighter and a half-smoked doobie containing The Blend. He lit the joint, and the Zippo's flame briefly converted the room's night blue into orange shadows. This revealed a tiny, noisy refrigerator, and a sink barely bigger than a mixing bowl. A hot plate was dangerously plugged to an extension cord hung from the ceiling.

Peckfogle stepped to the window so he could blow smoke through the grenade screen. He sucked down Blend smoke, and it felt good.

The Blend had the power to relieve Peckfogle of the Burden of History.

Peckfogle's paternal line had farmed a rocky, stubborn patch of Pennsylvania until his father had crossed the Delaware and married into Jersey Irish. By the rules of Pope Somebody, Peckfogle's mom, born Colleen Mannix, and all her children, were brought up Catholic, eating potatoes and farting copiously in an Irish slum.

Before their downturn into Shanty Catholic, the Peckfogles had a long history as Protestants, emphasis on the Protest. They had been forced into the margins of Pennsylvania Dutch Country as punishment for the crime of non-conformity. His father, a thundering tyrant at home, was a Professional Do-Gooder. He had last been arrested protesting the construction of a nuclear power plant at Three Mile Island, on behalf of the Society for the Preservation of Water Fowl. His mother had become an anti-war protestor the day her son had taken the Army oath. Aunt Jennifer Peckfogle had traveled the nation on behalf of the Equal Rights Amendment. His sister Dolly Madison Peckfogle had started her own religion, which the IRS was investigating as a tax dodge. His brother Benjamin Franklin Peckfogle had joined a California commune. In the long history of the Peckfogles, stretching back to the Holy Roman Empire, they were indifferent farmers, unceasing complainers, pesky neighbors and outrageous cheapskates. During the European civil wars of the late 1840s, the Peckfogle clan had opposed all factions, and had been expelled from Germany. Upon arrival in Baltimore, they filed a harassment complaint against U.S. Customs.

The Jersey Irish side of the Peckfogle family? Forget about it. Most Irish Catholics have the comfort of whiskey and beer, but Peckfogle's Irish in-laws were teetotalers, mourning the advent of birth control and the demise of Prohibition.

On the balcony of Merci's apartment, John Jay Peckfogle heard the unmistakable woosh-whump of a mortar round leaving the tube. He waited a beat. Was this the beginning of an attack on the base?

He craned his neck to watch the horizon through the heavy grenade screen. If this was an attack, that single round would cause hidden VC mortar-men to fire a barrage. These rounds would land in Long Binh with a heavy thump thump thump, causing panic, damage, injury, maybe even killing a few drunken Newbies.

The VC loved to aim for the casino, knowing it would be crowded all night.

But this time, no barrage. This was one thump, merely an illumination round, fired by GIs at Long Binh. Its parachute flare began drifting in the wind toward the city.

The floating flare cast harsh light and deep shadows all along Cong Ly Street. Looking through the mesh of the grenade screen, Peckfogle could see a ramshackle, trashy market street, lifeless except for half-starved stray dogs and Crocodile.

Sitting atop his idling yellow Honda, Crocodile, creature of the night, awaited a victim. If you were Vietnamese and foolish enough, or drunk enough, to be out at night, you belonged to Crocodile. He had never been known to directly attack a GI. Such a foolish act would entangle him with the MPs. But if you were local he would leave you broke and maybe knife-slashed to teach you a lesson. Certainly no women would venture out at night in Crocodile's neighborhood.

All the merchants paid Crocodile's "Street Tax," $55 if you had a storefront, and $11 if only a stall.

Many in the neighborhood bore the scars of an encounter with Crocodile. He preferred not to kill his victims. The dead, after all, are slow to pay their bills.

The parachute flare flickered out. Some merciless god threw the black blanket of night over Cong Ly Street. And again no one could see through the darkness.

The only sound was the puttering of Crocodile's motorbike.

CHAPTER THREE

In the morning I inspected my tattoo and applied another bandage.

It's made by Johnson & Johnson, a New Jersey company and quite the employer of Saint Sebastian's graduates. To get a job there, or at any prestige New Jersey company, it helped to be recommended by Sister Charles Borromeo.

Which meant you had to find algebra fascinating, wear madras shirts, chino trousers and desert boots, join the Sodality of the Blessed Virgin and memorize your Catechism.

Why did God make me?
God made me to know, love and serve Him in this world.

See?

Even in the Catechism, one-sentence paragraphs.

We Bayway Boys sneered at the Catechism.

We were destined to join the Army and bleed for our country.

Yes! The Collegiates would make the bandages, and the Bayway Boys would bleed.

Me, I'd rather bleed.

I am bitter, and that is my destiny as a Peckfogle.

Bitterness, the sages say, is frustrated love.

My friend Du Ky does not perceive me as bitter, since by his standards I am oozing luck.

Poor Du Ky, he keeps falling and can't hit bottom.

He's always at the tarot card reader's, hoping for a better Fate.

He doesn't understand her financial motivation. If he gets an optimistic forecast, he doesn't return. But when she forecasts doom, he'll be back soon with another $1, hoping to change his Fate.

I informed Du Ky of my Monetary Theory of Fate.

And he spit beer onto the road, laughing.

Apparently I do not understand the Tarot.

Last Tet, Du Ky finally wrenched together a spare-parts cyclo, only to have Crocodile tax him $55 for a license.

The cyclo only cost him $40 to build.

Last month he bought a crappy used Seiko watch, and a Saigon Cowboy drove by and ripped it off his wrist.

Last year, his girlfriend ran off to Bangkok with an Algerian construction worker.

Although Du Ky scorns my Tarot advice as American ignorance, I am such a valuable passenger that he will wait for hours at the Marilyn Monroe just to give me a ride to base.

I sometimes pay off in Blend cigarettes.

Du Ky likes The Blend.

Everybody likes The Blend.

Until they can't live without it.

And then they hate The Blend.

Du Ky flicked off his noisy engine so he could ask me about a movie that just hit Saigon: *Once Upon a Time in the West.*

I said I hadn't seen it.

"No?" He said. "But Henry Fonda!"

"Can we get going please? I'm sweating like a pig."

Du Ky drove me along the stinky river and over rusty bridges.

Those are the primary colors of this nation, the green of uniforms and jungle and the red of rust and dried blood.

Red is the color of good fortune in Vietnam. Green means bad luck.

Green and red! Everywhere!

Except for the traffic lights.

They've been dark since the War began.

Every intersection is either a rush-and-dare crossroads, or a suicidal traffic circle.

"Peck," Du Ky shouts over his shoulder, "we ride like John Wayne. Grab your balls!"

And then he weaves his filthy motorized spare-parts rickshaw through jeeps and trucks and scooters, scattering the occasional petrified pedestrian.

At Main Gate, the MPs smile for maybe the first time in their miserable shifts. They're obeying Colonel Sadler's orders, and keeping out the drugs even they crave.

They enforce the rules with pistols, clubs and German Shepherds.

I provide amusement for the MPs.

I provide them with a victim.

I provide them with a stark example of why they should obey regulations: Because otherwise, you end up scorned, like Peckfogle.

The MPs know the rules: Kiss ass, follow orders, worship Authority. But they tolerate me because I've been known to carry sticks of The Blend through the gate.

It's the price of admission.

It's why I have the rare privilege of living off base.

It works like this: However many MPs are on Main Gate duty, that's the number of sticks of The Blend that I carry through.

Du Ky tells me the magic number every morning.

He's my Main Gate Man.

The MPs shake me down, find the sticks, wag their fingers and say: *We'll let you go this time, Peckfogle.*

Because The Blend wears off.

And they'll need it again tomorrow.

The MPs love me when I am Doctor Blend, reliever of all ailments.

And despise Peckfogle, the druggie weakling.

I passed through the gate via this Holy Ritual and plodded down muddy Main Street toward my bunker at Graves Registration.

To get there I have to pass the Coffin Yard. There they lie, stacked in piles, awaiting the inevitable dead soldiers.

My bunker is a cool one, since I share a wall with a giant refrigerator, which is chilling the bodies of my fellow soldiers, packed in wood-and- aluminum caskets.

The building, one story and very long, makes an excellent mortar target, and has been hit twice, a waste of VC ordinance, really, since most of its occupants are dead.

The building was constructed of reject wood imported from Oregon by crooked American contractors and it announces its purpose on its outside: 165th Graves Registration, Finance and Accounting Unit.

Around the back is my little office, sandbagged against mortar attack, and without even a ray of sunlight. I sandbagged it myself, one sweaty bag at a time, using an entrenching tool to fill the green bags with rust-red Vietnamese earth.

With a flip of the light switch, I reveal my primary weapon: An Underwood manual typewriter.

Inside a steel box in my desk is my secondary weapon, a pack of The Blend.

I light a stick.

Pain, where is thy sting?"

Immediate flood of good feeling.

No wonder people pay $10 a stick.

Now, with The Blessed Blend coursing through my brain, I assume the duties of Army Professional Writer.

I lift a sheet of cheap mimeo paper out of the Underwood and read what I wrote yesterday.

> Dear Mr. and Mrs. Cameron
>
> Please accept with our deepest respect the belongings of your son Stewart. May they forever remind you of his honor and courage. Stewart (check spelling) was the bravest and finest young man it has ever been my privilege to command. He was the most popular man in our unit and will be sorely missed for his (pick one) ~~warm winning personality, good natured humor,~~ personal integrity.
>
> Stewart sacrificed his life during a military convoy that was bringing (pick one) relief to a besieged contingent of American soldiers ~~food to starving children~~. We know that his passing will bring great grief to you, his family, but pray that it will also bring lasting honor and glory, with the knowledge that he gave his life for a better world of freedom and democracy.
>
> Sincerely
>
> Captain Joseph P. Clark, United States Army.

Satisfied with last night's editing, I cracked my knuckles to warm up for re-typing.

Out of respect for the dead, I write the final drafts in standard paragraphs, although I do have to force it, and the result is not quite up to my usual Professional Writer standards of concision, brevity, clarity and dishonesty.

I am a Catholic-trained writer, Saint Sebastian be praised.

I have diagrammed a thousand sentences on the blackboard.

Subject! Verb! Object!

Easy on the exclamation points, Sister Charles, I can do it.

SOLDIER / IS / DEAD

See?

I've identified the object.

The object is death.

I was forced to take shorthand and typing at Saint Sebastian's because I rode a noisy red Triumph motorcycle to school, wore leather jackets, smoked Camels, drank at Mombo Bill's and mocked the nuns.

This was not the prelude to a Collegiate future.

The day Saint Sebastian's spit me out with a Secretarial degree, I set fire to the church.

It wasn't a big deal like it sounds, Your Honor.

Saint Sebastian's is still there, casting its moralistic shadow over Exit 13 of the Jersey Turnpike.

Even before the fire trucks pulled away from Saint Sebastian's, Sister Charles pointed the Finger of Blame at me.

The judge in that case, ~~may he squirm in hell~~, did not buy my claim that I had merely been lighting candles, praying for the release of my Peckfogle ancestors from Protestant Purgatory.

In a filthy office in the basement of the Union County Courthouse, with rat traps set under the lawyers' desks, my Public Defender gave me exactly three minutes of her time.

She had two words of advice.

Plea bargain!

Only a fool, she said, would stand trial in a New Jersey courtroom for a crime against the Catholic Church.

What crime? I said.

I was offered a deal worked out by Sister Charles and Judge Brendan Patrick O'Day : Five years in Rahway State Prison, or two years in the United States Army.

Yes drill sergeant!

The Army made me shout "kill kill" at Fort Dix and then it was machine guns at Fort Ord and then a new equation: Catholic schoolboy x 16 weeks of training = killing machine.

Upon arrival in the nation where we were Slaughtering Hearts and Minds, I solved the equation for X by going on sick call.

A lot.

Sick call was where sane people avoided ambush, day sweep or recon patrol.

When Captain Clark discovered I could type 40 words a minute, he requisitioned me for Graves Registration, and that's how I missed my chance to step on a Bouncing Betty, or be slaughtered via AK47.

All hail Captain Clark!

I ended up here, a writer of military fiction, horror genre, comforting the unfortunate parents of young men whose lives were cut short for no sensible purpose.

Somewhere on the other side of that cold wall, lay the body of Stewart Cameron.

He'd been out on routine convoy, driving point, in front of trucks that were supposed to deliver ammo, food and beer to the Arvin slouches at Rach Gia.

Yes, that's right, we bribed the Arvin with beer, hoping they'd be too drunk to run from combat, which was their main talent.

In all of combat history, no soldiers, not even the Arvin, ever abandoned a cache of ice cold beer.

All three of the GIs in Spec. 4 Cameron's convoy jeep were stoned on acid.

The driver flipped the jeep. There are no roll bars in those things, since the mounted machine gun takes their place.

Stewart Cameron, well, lets be respectful, okay?

It will be a closed coffin event back in Ohio.

Time to roll in the official Army letterhead and retype the letter to the Camerons.

Thank you Sister Charles for making me take typing.

In trying to crush my spirit you saved my life.

But this bandage is cramping my fingers, so it's gotta come off.

Since I've got Blend on the brain, I feel no pain in ripping the bandage.

I examine the tattoo, which is three distinct capital letters, inked in blue.

F T A

CHAPTER FOUR

Private Peckfogle carried a single cardboard box to the Long Binh Main Post Office. That building, constructed of gleaming concrete, stood out shiny and strong on a base of mud-spattered wooden shacks and barracks.

Peckfogle took a perverse pleasure in his duty as Personal Effects Specialist at Graves Registration. He suspected this assignment was the latest move in Colonel Sadler 's devious plan to destroy him. Sadler, commander of the MPs, was likely hoping that Peckfogle would steal the belongings of dead soldiers. Such a sacrilege would bring new charges that could send Peckfogle not just to LBJ, but to Leavenworth.

But Colonel Sadler was wrong about Peckfogle. He was no thief. He hated the Army but was sympathetic to his fellow sufferers, the common soldiers. In Peckfogle's warped mind, all soldiers were Designated Suckers. He took seriously his duty to treat their meager belongings with respect, to wrap them carefully, and to mail them to the shocked and bereaved parents, along with soothing fictions in the form of "commander's letters."

In a perverse way, Peckfogle found this duty satisfying. He could do nothing to alleviate the family's grief, but the mementos he mailed home would be treasured for a lifetime.

Peckfogle's favorite postal clerk was Spec. 4 Skinner, who manned the Parcels Window. The lucky Skinner worked in the safest building on base. The brass had sequestered him in its bowels because, like Peckfogle, Skinner was an embarrassment. In this clean-shaven Army, Skinner had the permanent shadow of a reddish beard.

The box Peckfogle set on the gleaming steel counter was addressed in careful block printing to the unfortunate Cameron family in Dayton, Ohio.

"Just one?" Skinner asked.

"Fuck the Army," said Peckfogle.

"Goes without saying," Skinner said.

Peckfogle saluted.

"What the fuck?"

"All due respect," said Peckfogle.

Skinner stared at the edge of Peckfogle's saluting hand, at the tattooed letters FTA.

"It stands for Fuck The Army," said Peckfogle.

"I know what it means," said Skinner. "Are you nuts?"

"Every time I salute an officer ..."

"You're going to prison."

"My ticket out of here," said Peckfogle.

"They'll put you back in LBJ."

"I've got a couple of cushy federal prison camps in mind, all of them back in The World. I hear they have tennis courts, soda machines and well-stocked libraries."

"Is that a permanent tattoo?"

"Mine for life."

"Have it inked over. Now. Today. How stoned were you?"

"I was Blended, actually."

"Fuck-O-Rama," said Skinner.

"Look, I'm on the edge of a deal downtown. Big, I mean, not just a couple of sticks. We're talking wholesale."

Skinner, picking up a well-chewed pencil, began writing a receipt for the box. "Get it inked over, Peck, all's I'm saying. This time, I'm not going to visit you in LBJ. Who was the sap?"

"Name was Cameron."

"I can see that," Skinner said, "I can read."

"Convoy to Rach Gia," Peckfogle said. "Fell out of a tumbling jeep."

"Stoned?"

"Lima Sierra Delta," said Peckfogle.

"Combat casualty then," said Skinner.

"Aren't we all?" said Peckfogle.

Peckfogle shook the box to assure himself it was packed right, and didn't rattle. Inside that box was a Pentax camera, a chess set with black-and-red pieces, a Bible and two comic books: *Justice League of America* and *Sgt. Fury!* There were letters from Cameron's girlfriend that Peckfogle had wrapped, without reading them, in clear plastic. There was a multi-band radio and a photo album of soldiers, almost all of them black fellows. Peckfogle had not known this GI or much about him, except that he'd been a jeep gunner and was now dead and his parents lived in Dayton, Ohio. Peckfogle had elected not to include the dead man's watch, which had been shattered when he hit the ground. Nor could his portable TV be shipped. So Peckfogle had sold that TV to Miss Hanh, his hooch maid. He included the proceeds, three worn $5 bills, in an envelope inside the box.

"So, no go on the court martial?" Skinner asked, and slid the box down a steel chute.

"Lucky me," said Peckfogle. "Their best witness went down in a Slick, right into the Mekong."

"Drowned?"

"Sergeant Slaughter. MIA. Never found him."

"Fuck-O-Rama," said Skinner. "Feeding the fishes in the South China Sea."

Skinner looked up and down the long counter, where clerks, all male, all dressed in olive-drab fatigues, lounged amid sacks and carts.

"Visit me tonight," said Skinner.

"Tower duty?"

"Twenty three," said Skinner. "My name is Mister Jones. Bring our friend."

"The cupboard is bare," said Peckfogle.

"Come anyway," said Skinner, and rubbed his stubbly face. "It's a good place to talk," he whispered, and looked over his shoulder. "Too many ears around here, all's I'm saying."

In southern Vietnam, days and nights were of more or less equal length. The sun set not long after six, and Army mess halls closed at sundown. Every dinner time, Peckfogle checked the menu posted on the mess hall's screen doors. Almost every day he was disappointed. Macaroni and cheese was the only entree item he could eat, and even then, he had to pick out the ham. So on this day, as he so often did, he retreated to his dark, sandbagged room just off the mortuary, and chose from his stockpile of food: Ramen noodles from the PX, and items filched from C-rations: canned fruit and cake, tins of peanut butter and olive-drab packs of crackers.

It was lonely, being a vegetarian in the Army. It was lonely being a True Believing Lapsed Catholic in the Army. It was lonely being the only mosquito-wings private in Vietnam. Even the lowest newbie was a PFC the moment he stepped off the plane. Two grades higher than Peckfogle! Clearly, the Army's strategy was to isolate and humiliate Peckfogle, whose unforgivable crime was to mock authority.

He really couldn't help it. Genetic destiny! Snakes slither, birds fly, and Peckfogles defy authority.

And once he removed that bandage, every time he saluted an officer, he'd send a Peckfoglian message: Fuck The Army.

He wouldn't last a day once the bandage came off.

Perhaps in another war, the Army's solution would have been to discharge Peckfogle. But the U.S. Army in Vietnam was composed largely of draftees who wanted desperately to go home. A Peckfogle discharge would open an easy way out for other dissidents. Tattoo parlors would be besieged by soldiers seeking FTA inkings.

Peckfogle had already served time at LBJ for the crime of Refusing to Consume C-Rations.

C-rations contained no vegetarian meals, so Peck, in his infantry days, refused to carry them. His sergeant, Joe Slaughter, yes that really was his name, wrote him up for Endangering a Combat Mission. Eating only Saltines during a 3-day patrol made Peckfogle weak and unfit for combat, Sergeant Slaughter complained. That endangered his fellows on ambush patrol. It was a six-man stealth patrol that needed every alert rifle it could get.

So Peckfogle ended up in front of a review board headed by Colonel Sadler, strack commander of the MPs.

Peckfogle was judged to be an insubordinate and self-righteous maggot and therefore worthy of a General Courts Martial.

The fundamental charge was Harm to Government Property, i.e. himself.

There's a lot of idle time in any Army, which breeds gossip and speculation. Some GIs theorized that the Army was purposely dragging out Peckfogle's trial. The point was to show all the other draftees what happened to a soldier who dared to defy the Brass.

Perhaps the worst punishment was this: The days Peckfogle spent in LBJ did not count toward his 365. All around him GIs were working off their 365-day sentence. But Peckfogle was in Vietnam Limbo, waiting for the Adjutant to officially drop the charges, and until then his countdown clock stood still.

His miserable, slumping form, seen all around the base, was a warning to all who would defy authority.

Poor guy, the other GIs whispered, he'll be in Vietnam forever.

After his dinner of ramen, peanut butter and a Tums, Peckfogle walked to Skinner's tower. In the lowering dusk he passed a gaggle of Newbies, in their tell-tale dark uniforms, outside their barracks. They were engaged in a game of horseshoes, four guys playing and the rest of them betting. Close only counts in hand grenades and horseshoes, they say. These Newbies would soon exchange those horseshoes for hand grenades.

They were smoking cigarettes, laughing and drinking canned soda as the sun set behind them. They stood in clusters, self-segregated into Latino, Black and White. A few of them might be dead next week, their bodies at Graves Registration, their belongings wrapped up by Peckfogle and mailed home in a box.

Peckfogle waved at SSG Foster, Minder of Newbies, who sat sweating in the shade beside a huge purple cooler adorned with a PEPSI logo. The sergeant's duty was to prevent the Newbie barracks from breaking out into a race riot. His side job was selling Pepsis to overheated Newbies. His criminal activity was selling sticks of The Blend to anxious Newbies, at the much inflated price of $25.

Occasionally Peckfogle had sold Foster a few stray sticks of The Blend, hence the friendly wave.

Peckfogle, out of uniform, in the dread heat, walked the concertina wire in the shadow of Long Binh Jail. The sight of that stalag made him shudder, and he looked away.

His light-hearted disdain for LBJ was a façade. He'd almost lost his mind in there. His sadistic guards at LBJ delivered his dinner tray with a punch to the face. The most sadistic guard learned he was in for the crime of being a vegetarian and delivered disgusting all-meat dinners.

LBJ housed its inmates not in cells but in olive drab steel shipping cubes. Every day in that container Peckfogle expected to die of heat stroke. He lost twelve pounds in there, existing on bread, potatoes and soggy string beans. In desperation, he had pretended that the Army's powdered eggs were so de-natured that they were vegan.

Tower 23 was spot-lit bright. Peckfogle put one foot on the wooden ladder and called up.

"Skinner?"

"Advance and be recognized," said a voice from behind the spotlight.

"Lifer talk," grumbled Peckfogle, and climbed the ladder.

He hoisted himself up through a trap door and then it was just him and Skinner behind the spotlight. Skinner pulled tower guard duty twice a week. Peckfogle saw this as Lifer punishment for Skinner's shaving profile. A clean shave every day was gospel in the Army, but because he had chronic skin irritation, Skinner was allowed to shave every third day. This gave him a haunted, unmilitary look, offset by–wary gray eyes. Skinner had to carry his medical profile papers everywhere. He was constantly stopped by officers who wanted to demand that he shave. After months of this hectoring, he'd joined Peckfogle in hatred of the Army.

Skinner was a young man, but his fingers were knobby and wrinkled like an old farmer's. He'd grown up in some prairie town, milking cows.

"You come loaded, dude?" asked Skinner.

"Empty," said Peckfogle, and turned out one pocket of his cut-offs.

"Fuck-O-Rama," said Skinner. "What good are you?"

Skinner paced the tower, which was just big enough to sleep four men in cots. The tower looked out over 100 yards of minefield laced with concertina wire, and then a swamp, and in the distance, a Vietnamese village, and then Bien Hoa Air Base. Mounted dead center in the tower, and facing that minefield, was a black M-60 machine gun with shiny brass ammo snaking out of its breach. Over the tower wall hung gray Claymore clackers. With one squeeze, they could set off a blast that would kill everything within a hundred yards.

"Jonesing for a stick," said Skinner.

"You and the whole base," said Peckfogle.

"Brought to you in living Fuck-O-Rama."

"Got a plan," said Peckfogle.

"I figured," said Skinner.

"Fifty five cartons," Peckfogle said.

"Salems? Kools? What?"

"You know."

Skinner whistled. "Insane, man."

"One duffle bag."

"You'll be a fucking legend, all's I'm saying. You got a line on this shit?"

"I need cash, good faith money, five thousand."

"Way over my head," said Skinner, pacing. He stopped to stare out at the barbed wire minefield. "Shit, I'm not General Westmoreland. I get $180 on payday."

"Plus combat pay, plus overseas pay. Come on, man, you been saving for an Impala since Day One."

"Peckfogle, did you like LBJ? Is that it? You want to go back?"

"We split $5000 profit after the deal closes. A year's pay for you, man, that's a fortune over here."

Skinner, scouting the swamp with binoculars, said: "How do you get 55 cartons through the ... Hey! Movement."

"What are you talking about?"

"Victor Foxtrot Charley."

"Give me those," said Peckfogle. He snatched the binoculars and scanned the minefield. After a long moment he said: "Nothing."

"Fuck-O-Rama," said Skinner. "Are you blind? I'm gonna blow guard."

Skinner picked up an aluminum flare tube, uncapped it, and jammed it against his thigh. A white streak hissed out of it and headed for the sky. It became a parachute flare and drifted over the minefield.

"Blow a claymore," said Skinner.

"No way man."

"Blow one asshole!"

"I'm on probation, I'm a noncombatant."

"Coward," said Skinner. He put his shoulder into the machine gun, sighted down the barrel, flicked the safety off and fired. As he swiveled the chattering gun, a long burst of red tracer rounds flew every which way over the minefield. Peckfogle put on a helmet and held his fingers in his ears.

Skinner fired another long burst, the brass snake of ammo whipping through the gun and flinging hot brass everywhere, a few empty shells bouncing off Peckfogle's helmet. Tower 24 began firing and then tower 25. The assault siren began wailing.

"God bless America!" cried Skinner. "Take that, Charley!"

Somebody back in the mortar pit began firing illumination rounds. A searchlight beam began crisscrossing the minefield. As the illumination rounds burned out, a searchlight helicopter lifted away from the distant airfield, red navigation light blinking.

Every tower was now firing, a bright-red withering assault that no enemy could possibly survive. Claymore mines exploded in blinding, booming flashes. Sirens wailed. A truck full of reaction force soldiers roared up and squeaked to a stop at the base of the tower. Angry men with rifles rushed out.

Skinner loaded a new belt into his M-60.

"Ain't war a blast?" shouted Skinner. "Change the barrel for me, will you, Peck? It's red hot man. There's the mitts."

Peckfogle saw a jeep full of MPs racing toward the tower, and an idea was born. He was so struck by this idea that he ignored Skinner's request.

Skinner changed the barrel on the machine gun and said, "Come on, Peck, blow a claymore before they call cease fire. Let's have some fun. Fuck-O-Rama."

Reaction force soldiers, in helmets and body armor, began climbing up to reinforce the towers. MPs parked their jeeps at the wire and scrambled out.

"I've got it," said Peckfogle.

"What did you say?" asked Skinner.

"I've got a plan now." Peckfogle squeezed the clacker and blew a Claymore.

His ears would ring for days.

CHAPTER FIVE

When Merci heard the snap-snap-snap of a distant fire fight, she climbed the ladder to the roof. From this perspective, three stories up, she could see over the rooftops, the town, the roads, the river all dark. It was only the U.S. Army Base at Long Binh that glowed.

At Long Binh searchlight helicopters circled. Occasional bursts of red tracer fire arced from the helicopters into the darkness. Merci, feeling dizzy, let her hand rest on the brick parapet. She took a breath and told herself this firefight was nothing. There were no green VC tracers being fired back at the GIs. Another panic firefight, GIs against the Ghosts.

She heard Mr. Tin climbing the ladder. She could tell it was him by the soft sound of his slippers on the wooden steps. Mr. Tin, like many Vietnamese, preferred to be known to the GIs by a nickname. Real names were deeply connected to family, and not to be shared with dirty foreigners.

The old man did not approach Merci immediately but veered off to check on his pigeons. These were not for racing or homing, but to sell in the food market. He kept them in a big cage, partly covered by a dark tarp. Mr. Tin's approach caused them to coo. He cooed back at them, and called them pretty. By the time he stood alongside Merci at the parapet, the bright commotion at the Army base had faded to dark silence.

He was a weak old man, barely able to climb the ladder now, and Merci imagined the day when he could no longer get up here to feed his pigeons. Standing next to Merci, he smelled of stale tobacco and strong tea. He looked toward her with clouded eyes. Half-blinded by cataracts, Mr. Tin was descending into a world of murky light and shadow.

Have you eaten, daughter? he said.

I am waiting for my American, she said.

He is very peculiar, said Mr. Tin. *They are a most peculiar people, daughter, and that is all I have to say. To you, and to my birds, safe night.*

Safe night, uncle, said Merci.

As she listened to him climb down the ladder, she felt a shudder of loneliness. She watched the dark Cong Ly Street with small hope. Unless Peckfogle had left the base just before the firefight, he would not be arriving tonight. If his rickshaw taxi did not pull up in a minute or two, Peckfogle would not be coming.

The only light on Cong Ly Street tonight came from the Marilyn Monroe, the café favored by Crocodile. It was rare to see a Vietnamese soldier in the Marilyn Monroe after dark.

The café's evening trade was provided by GIs and their local girlfriends. Mr. Tin was right, the Americans were a peculiar people. They were very slow to realize that the VC had changed strategy. In Bien Hoa they were not trying so much to kill Americans as to sap them of their dollars. This money was used to finance the fighting in other provinces, where the VC had more hope for victory. Every beer the Americans drank on Cong Ly Street helped the VC. Every time they paid a prostitute, tipped a masseuse, consumed a bowl of noodles, bought a shirt, or rode in a cyclo-taxi, they were funding their enemies. Here on this street, Crocodile was the middle man between American money and the Viet Cong.

Some GIs seemed to vaguely understand this, but many did not.

Merci gave up on spotting Peckfogle, descended the ladder and locked herself into her room. It had no glass in the windows, just two screens: a fine one for mosquitoes and a thick one on the balcony for hand grenades. She watched out those screens as true darkness settled on Cong Ly Street. A gas-powered generator on the street sputtered, and her overhead light winked out. Apartments across the street also went dark, although some glowed with weak candle light.

She ate a dinner of cold spicy eggplant and rice that she meant to share with Peckfogle. She had not seen Crocodile on the street. There was a chance he would not be aware of Peckfogle's absence, and might leave her in peace. By the time she had washed the dinner pot, fear had worn itself down past resignation and into hope

And then she heard steps in the hallway. A scratch, like a cat scratch, sounded at the door. She lit a fat candle and carried it to the door. She opened, it, stepped back, and admitted Crocodile.

Where's your GI? he asked.

He was a small man, but wiry and strong, cat-like and quick, a vicious soccer player and dangerous street fighter in his youth. The two sides of his face did not match, one almost immobile with a weepy ruined eye.

She retreated to the kitchen table, set down the candle, fished in it for money, finding only American MPC. When she handed the crumpled blue bills to Crocodile he said: *No greenbacks?*

She shook her head.

She owed him $55 a month in protection money but on nights when Peck wasn't around, Crocodile would knock for a "tip."

He put a cigarette in his lips. Merci lit it with a candle and smelled a hint of singed hair.

If you are going to kill me tonight, she said, *I would like to leave a note for my mother.*

Why would I destroy such a useful specimen?

He tapped cigarette ashes onto the tabletop.

The candle trembled in Merci's hand.

Where is your GI? he asked.

Coming later, she said.

Crocodile laughed. *You go through them so quickly.*

He bent to open and inspect her refrigerator.

He doesn't drink beer? Tell me, what is his task in the beehive?

I believe he sends home the belongings of dead GIs. Their watches and other valuable things.

I hope he stays very busy then. What do you have for me today? What gossip do they reveal when your girls have their dicks in hand?

Everyone seems nervous. There is talk of Cambodia.

There is always talk of Cambodia. What else?

I can think of no more.

What was all that noise after sundown?

How would I know? I was here watching from the rooftops.

With your reactionary landlord.

Yes.

And the traitor he calls his son?'

His son is away. Before you ask, I don't know.

What is your GI's weakness?

He smokes your Blend.

I believe he and I will do business before I destroy him.

Merci shrugged. *I cannot stop you, Crocodile.*

Perhaps he has doubts, so suggest to him that Crocodile is a good man for business.

Of course I'll do it, said Merci.

Crocodile dropped his khaki shorts around his ankles. He wore no underwear. He pulled a curved knife from its scabbard and said: *Please me.*

Merci dipped a gray dishrag in a bowl of rinse-water, stepped toward Crocodile and dropped to her knees. With that dishrag she washed his flaccid dirty penis.

Gentle, said Crocodile. *As you would treat a baby.*

He lay the knife on the table, just inches from her head.

He said: *The knife is there. Go ahead and kill me, as you have long desired. Slice my throat, you coward.*

She looked up at him. *I am not made of your flesh, Crocodile.*

He laughed. *Honor stands and cowardice kneels. It is that simple. Kneel coward and take me in.*

Merci took his limp penis in her mouth. Despite her washing, it tasted of filth. It was known on the street that he had lost his abilities as a man, and this fact Merci kept in her heart as revenge.

I offered you my knife, Crocodile said, *and you chose to suck me instead.*

She backed away. She stood as Crocodile raised his shorts. She picked up the knife in trembling hand. She held the blade and offered it, handle first, toward him.

Go! she said.

He did not know about the little pistol she kept hidden in the jug of rice. She didn't need his knife if she wanted to kill him.

All your GI boyfriends, said Crocodile. He spit on her floor. *And none can protect you.*

CHAPTER SIX

Skinner pulled up at the Marilyn Monroe in a shiny jeep. It may have been the only shiny jeep in all of muddy Bien Hoa. He parked two wheels on the sidewalk, forcing pedestrians to squeeze between jeep and café tables. An M-16 strapped over his shoulder, Skinner walked past tables crowded with uniformed GIs and Arvins. At the counter, he slapped Peckfogle on the back.

"There's two kinds of coffee," Skinner said. "Army coffee and real coffee. You prick. Another benefit of living off base."

Peckfogle grunted.

"You're probably getting laid twice a night," Skinner said. "Maybe I need to get court martialed, so I can live the good life too."

From behind a half-sandbagged wall, Sanny appeared, backing through the curtain with bowls of rice porridge in either hand. She of the pretty pale face and long stringy hair allowed a tight smile for Peckfogle.

"Kinda young," said Skinner. "Fuck-O-Rama man, don't you have scruples?"

Skinner's three-day growth of dark red hair only partly hid his chronic facial rash. When he lay his boonie hat on the tile counter, he revealed a severe butch haircut and big floppy ears.

"Order!" demanded Sanny.

"Bacon and eggs," said Skinner.

"Bacon, we don't have!"

"Eggs then."

"Out of eggs!"

"What you got, then?"

"Rice gruel," said Peckfogle.

"*Chao*," said Sanny.

"They're out of everything but rice and coffee," said Peckfogle.

"We get nothing today," claimed Sanny.

"The horrors of war," said Skinner.

"Rice porridge," said Peckfogle, and belched. "Good for the digestion."

"Okay, bowl of *chao*," said Skinner. "And coffee, the good coffee, not that instant crap you serve the Arvins."

Sanny disappeared behind the beaded curtains, whick whick.

"Doesn't she work at your steam joint?" Skinner asked.

"It's not my steam joint."

"But she works there right?"

"Only when they're super busy."

"What is she, fifteen?"

"I have no idea. She's some kind of niece to the landlord."

"She gives hand jobs at fifteen?"

"Ask Merci, I don't have anything to do with it, I'm in enough trouble as it is."

Skinner looked around. "This place is a death trap. They got a back door? Somebody rolls a frag in here, we're all blown to shit."

Peckfogle pointed to the sandbags that lined the bottom two feet of the counter and were stacked along the kitchen wall.

Skinner set his M-16 atop that counter. "You're down here with no sidearm, man?"

"I'm on restriction."

"So what?" He spread his arms. "We're in the world's most active weapons market. Buy something on the street."

"Merci's got a little handgun stashed at home."

Their conversation was interrupted when Crocodile's yellow motorcycle pulled up between the café and Skinner's jeep. Crocodile borrowed an Arvin soldier's .45, and flash-bam shot Skinner's jeep.

The right front tire blew out. With a hiss the Jeep sagged, and Crocodile puttered away in a cloud of blue smoke.

"Fuck-O-Rama!" shouted Skinner. He grabbed his M-16 and pushed past the tables and out into the sunshine. He sighted down the rifle but the yellow motorcycle had weaved into traffic.

Skinner pointed his rifle at the sky, turned toward the café and scowled at the soldiers. Some of the GIs, and more of the Arvins, were laughing at him.

Even the simple act of changing a tire was sweaty work, and Skinner was in a nasty mood as they drove down Cong Ly Street. Skinner, like just about every other driver on the chaotic street, honked his way through traffic, then through the traffic circle, until Long Binh Army Base came in sight. It was a tangled mass of concertina wire and guard towers that resembled a city-size prison.

Skinner pulled up at Main Gate and said: "I catch that dirty motherfucker what's his name?"

"Crocodile."

"You tell that prick..."

"Hey, that's what you get for parking like an American. I hate to tell you Skinner, but Crock's our man."

"What do you mean our man?"

"For the deal. He's the guy we were supposed to meet. I think blowing out your tire was a negotiating tactic."

"How's that?"

"A message. On Cong Ly Street, he does anything he pleases."

"What kind of assholes you dealing with, Peck?"

"The kind that can get 55 cartons of The Blend."

"Who makes that shit anyway?"

Peckfogle shrugged.

"There's a factory somewhere, right?" Skinner said. "We should find out. Deal direct. Cut out the psycho middleman."

A scowling silent MP walked around the jeep inspecting it, jotting a note onto his clipboard. When he walked back to the guardhouse, Peckfogle said: "What happened when we cut loose from Tower 23?"

"*We* cut loose? I remember you standing there like bozo the clown."

"It was like a big game of pinball, right? You tilt the machine, all the marbles rush to one side, right?"

Behind them a shit-stinking honey wagon pulled up, headed in to clean latrines and transport GI turds out into the boonies for burning.

"So Skinner, all's you gotta do is blow Tower 23. Perfect timing, I drive up to the main gate. Firefight! Contact at Tower 23. Panic! The guards shoo in all the GIs waiting out here, right? GI Joe running all over the place. Sirens, helicopters, parachute flares. I just happen to be at the gate with a sack of dope when you start ripping. Sundown. Perfect timing. In I go."

"And if it don't work?"

"They're not going to leave GIs on the wrong side of the gate during a firefight, man."

Their conversation paused as a scowling MP stomped past.

"And if it don't work?"

"I'll put it in reverse," Peckfogle said, "and try something else. Maybe I walk it through a carton at a time."

"There was a reason they slammed you into LBJ, man."

"Sadler has this place sealed even tighter than his asshole. You want to double your money or not?"

"I don't want to end up in LBJ."

"Man, they can't implicate you. You'll be up in the tower on guard duty when I slip through the gate. How would you know there's a load of dope at Main Gate? You seen movement out in the wire. Hey, think of that Chevy Impala. What color? Rag top? Cruising down the streets of where are you from?"

"Normal."

"No what town."

"Normal, man. It's a burg in Illinois."

"Okay, Normal, summer day, two babes in front, two babes in back, couple of reefers. Man, the girls of Normal are going to love that Impala ragtop."

"Shit, I always wanted to fight this war. Tower guard at Long Binh, that's the closest I'm ever gonna get. You'd see more combat as a security guard at K-Mart. I put in for the DMZ, up where they're kicking ass. And what do they do to me? Post office."

"The army finds out what you want, and makes you do the exact opposite. Don't you know that, Skin? Never tell your commander what you really want. If you really want to fight, they make you a post office REMF. If you're a scared shitless coward, they send you to the DMZ."

Peckfogle patted Skinner's shoulder. "It don't take a genius to figure this Army."

CHAPTER SEVEN

Mr. Tin, elderly widower, and landlord of #22 and #24 Cong Ly Street, lived in the apartment just above Merci's, third floor above the steam-bath. It was a very neat and clean apartment.

He lit incense in a brass pot before a framed photo of his dead son. On either side of that photo stood a flower vase and a gold-engraved plate. Curled photos of Mr. Tin's parents and grandparents were propped up amid a gray teapot and tiny cups. Mr. Tin moved a miniature bottle of wine, which would never be tasted, in front of the photo of his son.

They say it is changing, said Crocodile. *The youth of this country is celebrating birthdays now. Such ego! Soon we will all be Americans, Mr. Tin, don't you agree?*

Mr. Tin bowed to the altar, which was set upon his finest piece of furniture, a dark, shiny chest-of-drawers imported from Malaysia.

Crocodile sat at Mr. Tin's dining table, which was set low, just barely off the ground. Behind him hung an elaborate calendar enumerating the days of the Year of the Dog.

I meant to ask about Quang, Crocodile said. *I hear he is a sergeant now. He must be a good son. Oh, I love the aroma of aloeswood, Mr. Tin.*

Mr. Tin shuffled into his kitchen, opened a metal box, counted money, and brought the bills out to lay them on the table before Crocodile.

With his stubby fingers, Crocodile separated the bills into two piles.

Nobody wants piasters, he said. *It is a shame. I can only accept dollars now, Mr. Tin, so you shall owe me on account. You see, the Americans have made both ourselves and our currency worthless.*

Mr. Tin's gray cat peered around a corner, retreated.

Crocodile buttoned the greenbacks into the pocket of his GI-surplus olive drab shirt.

Perhaps I shall die before I see the fabled America. What must it be like in the land of magic money, Mr. Tin? Also, even their children drive automobiles, I've been told.

From the other shirt pocket he produced a wrinkled cigarette.

"*It is loyalty that counts, it does not matter the cause.*" He lit the cigarette, inhaled, closed his eyes. "*I do understand that a respectable landlord like yourself fears the Communists. We are not so bad as they say. But I do not blame your son for loyalty to this putrid government. One does what one must to survive.*"

He held out the burning cigarette, which Mr. Tin took and smoked.

I take it the café is earning good profits yet?

Mr. Tin shrugged.

I am thinking of trading in the gold in my teeth, said Crocodile. *Can you believe that? They can do that today, a miracle in the dental chair. In return for your gold they will give you an entire set of removable white teeth.*

He grinned.

Imagine me without my golden smile. So … the Negro whore downstairs has a new GI. … but I like the feeling of a mouth full of gold. Don't you think it makes a distinctive look on a man? Tell me what do you think of this new GI, Peckfogle? Does he know anything? I see there are some days he wears no uniform.

Mr. Tin returned only a forced smile.

Do not feel singled out, grandfather, said Crocodile. *The Marilyn Monroe is quite the healthy business, and only pays the standard tax. Everyone pays tribute equally, and all goes to Uncle Ho. I keep nothing for my humble self. No matter where your current loyalties lie, no matter what crimes your traitorous son commits, Ho is the whole nation's uncle. Did he not free us of the evil Japanese?*

Mr. Tin bent to set an empty tea cup on the table before Crocodile.

No tea, thank you, it is a vile beverage foisted upon us by our Chinese oppressors. What is it about our poor nation, Mr. Tin, why does every nation on earth wish to humiliate us? I would like to go to America just to spit on the shores. Who are these bastards to drop bombs on our country? To take our land for their bases. Vietnam has always been a poor, small country, a victim country, it is one mouse of a nation squeezed between elephants, don't you agree, grandfather?

Mr. Tin, in shaky hands, passed the opium-marijuana cigarette back to Crocodile. The GIs called this mixture "The Blend" and it could be quite addicting, with its power to kill pain. Crocodile poured himself a cup of tea and rested it on the kitchen counter. He finished the cigarette, and put it out by smashing its burning end into the varnished top of Mr. Tin's precious table.

So tell me, what do you know about this GI? Crocodile demanded.

The new one?

Of course. The one who sleeps with the treacherous old whore.

I call him head-in-the-clouds.

Why is that?

He has the look of a dreamer. And he smokes your Blend incessantly.

So many of them do.

Mr. Tin backed up to a Sanyo rice cooker. He unplugged it from an elaborate system of electric wires that all fed into one outlet.

I love the smell of steamed rice, Crocodile said. *It is the aroma of childhood, grandfather. Is he trustworthy, this new GI? Has the whore paid the rent on time since getting her hooks into him? Ah, my first smells in this world, mother's tit and warm rice.*

He spit on the floor.

Opium smoke, it is essential but it fouls the taste buds, Mr. Tin. I'm surprised you have an appetite for fine food, given how much you smoke. Why do I do it Mr. Tin? Oh, there's your cat atop the counter, flicking its vile tail. Have you caught any mice today, useless cat? I look at your cat and I wish to squash his head. Why do you think that is?

Mr. Tin set the cover on the incense burner, and a tiny final huff of aloeswood smoke escaped.

You are a quiet man, Mr. Tin. What are you keeping to yourself? Wisdom, I suspect. Wisdom, that rare gift.

Crocodile coughed and spit blood and saliva on Mr. Tin's tile floor.

I see a drunken Arvin staggering down the street, and I wish to drag him into the alley and disembowel him. I see a girl and I wish to humiliate her, to knock her down and piss on her. Why do I have these impulses? I don't know. Because when I gaze into the mirror I see a good and kind man. Have I been fair to you, grandfather? Tell me the truth."

"You have been most cordial."

"Even as I mar your table and spit vile fluids on your floor?"

Mr. Tin, at the kitchen counter, fussed preparing two plates. *"You are Crocodile. You have purpose, because beneath the appearances, all is harmony."*

"You understand me, grandfather, I suspect. I wish to destroy. I feel I must destroy. I am constantly looking for victims and they ... it is only the weak and soft that I prey upon, and it is their fault, it is their very cowardice ... Ah rice and pickles, thank you, I have such trouble with my bowels ... You see, grandfather, it is cowardice itself I wish to destroy."

He ignored the chopsticks and ate like a barbarian, scooping rice and pickles with his forefinger.

"You and your traitor son have nothing to fear from Crocodile. I can sense a coward, and you are bravery itself, grandfather. This new GI, head-in-the-clouds. Would you judge him a weak man or strong man, grandfather?"

Crocodile propped his elbows on the table and grinned.

"That is what I thought."

CHAPTER EIGHT

The son-of-a-bitch John Adams Peckfogle, do-gooder hypocrite, wrote me a letter even though I'd asked him to leave me be.

The letter came special delivery from my Post Office buddy and partner in drug conspiracy, Spec. 4 Skinner, aka Skin, aka Red Beard.

Skinner found me sitting alone in the mess hall, spreading rancid peanut butter on the Army's version of Wonder Bread.

The Vietnamese bake the most delicious baguettes this side of Paris, but the Army feeds us fortified factory fodder meant to Build Brave Bodies 8 ways.

I'm sure there's a slimy government contractor at the end of the white-bread supply chain.

Probably my old man's an investor in it.

That's his style, making money off other people's labor.

"Maybe your Dad sent you money," Skinner suggested, and set down the shit-brown envelope and a Bakelite mug of cold black vile Army coffee.

"You don't know John Adams Peckfogle," I said. "Growing up, I had to pay *him* an allowance."

That got no response from Skinner, so I said: "I sold skin magazines."

"As a kid?"

"Rode the bus to New York Port Authority, bought copies of Screw, Satan and Frenchie and sold 'em for double on the gritty streets of Bayway."

"They didn't have smut in your hometown?"

"You ever heard of the Legion of Decency?"

Skinner shook his head.

"Catholic mafia," I said. "They patrolled the magazine racks of Catholic cities like Bayway, determined to eliminate the Near Occasions of Sin."

"The what?"

"Never mind."

"Thank God I was raised atheist."

"That is lucky."

"So you're a born wheeler-dealer," said Skinner.

"Had to survive, the old man demanded $4 a week."

"Or else?"

"The Stick."

"Stick?" Skinner said. "Explain that."

"Nope."

"Aren't you going to open the letter?"

I picked up the envelope and flexed it, very thin, of course, since John Adams Peckfogle would never spring for double postage.

"He probably wrote to remind me that I caused all my own troubles by setting fire to a church."

"You burned down a church?"

"They exaggerated."

"Who exaggerated?"

"Sister Charles and the New Jersey Superior Court."

"A nun named Charles? Wow."

"It really isn't a superior court, by the way, it's run by the county's political hacks. Superior is just a name."

"A fragment of speech," Skinner said.

"And the church? It was barely singed."

"So that's how you ended up in This Man's Army."

"How about you, Skinner?"

"I joined to kill gooks."

"You joined? You're not a draftee?"

"My grandfather killed Krauts, my father bombed Japs, my uncle slaughtered Chinks, so I'm gonna kill me some Gooks."

"Why would you want to do that?"

He shrugged. "It's in the blood, all's I'm saying."

"What did the Viets ever do to you?"

"Fuck a bunch of Commies. Better here than on the beaches of Malibu."

He sat back in his stiff chair.

"You ever been to Mailbu?" I asked.

"California? Fuck no. Nothing but long-hair hippies."

"I'm going to live there some day."

Skinner spit into the coffee cup. "Fuck-O-Rama. I hate a Third World ass country. I just want to collect my souvenir gook and go home."

A small wizened Vietnamese man, about 60 years old, approached to wipe the table.

He was the Dining Room Orderly, one of hundreds of locals the Army had hired in an effort to Bribe Hearts and Minds.

"Why not shoot this old busboy and get it over with?" I asked Skinner.

The old man wiped the table with a vinegar-stinking rag.

"Because he ain't a Commie," Skinner said. "He has a job. Commies wear black pajamas, throw hand grenades at innocent GIs and don't have jobs. All's they know is government handouts."

"But you take a government handout every payday, right?"

"That's different," said Skinner. He snatched the man's skinny wrist. "You're no Commie, right, old timer?"

The old man, not comprehending, grinned.

Skinner let him go with shove of contempt.

"VC spy, all's I'm saying."

I tore one end off the envelope, pinched out the letter, and read.

"Dear Peckfogle ..."

Skinner scrambled to look over my shoulder.

"That's what he calls you? Not son, not my boy, not John Jay?"

"Nope. And he's the one who named me. For the first Chief Justice of the United States."

"Who?"

"A historical figure. Colonial times. Founding Father. You know."

Skinner patted his fatigue shirt, trying to locate his cigarettes.

"Skinner don't mess with history," he said, "and history don't mess with Skinner. Continue, oh genius."

"I'm afraid I have some bad news."

"Oh boy," said Skinner, and popped a Salem into his lips and rubbed his hands together.

"Your mother has been arrested in Idaho."

"Idaho?"

"I am not bailing her out this time, because she needs to learn her lesson."

"This time?" Skinner lit his cigarette with a lighter emblazoned with the likeness of John Wayne.

"You may have time to send her a Mother's Day card, at the Pocatello Women's Correctional Center, 1451 Fore Road."

"How cool!" said Skinner and blew smoke. "I wish I had a mom in prison. I'd write a country song. She's not in for whoring, is she?"

"A scathing account concerning the activities of your mother and her peacenik friends appeared last week on page B4 in the New York Times, embarrassing the entire family."

"New York Times," said Skinner. "My mom was in the Normal Pantagraph once."

"What'd she do?"

"Baked a blue ribbon pie."

"It had ribbons in it?"

Skinner cocked his head at me.

"That's a joke, Skinner."

He said: "What part of America are you from, anyway?"

"It's not really America. It's a wholly-owned oil-producing subsidiary called the Bayway Refinery."

"The what?"

"I gotta go."

"And do what?"

"Answer this letter."

"Hey, I gotta tell you, good news from Normal."

"Oh?"

"I wrote my mom and told her we could make some money. My mom's an investor at the thousand dollar level."

CHAPTER NINE

"Iced coffee," said Crocodile. "Thank you, Sanny."

They sat at a scarred table in the darkest corner in the Marilyn Monroe: Crocodile, Skinner and Peckfogle.

"The coffee and milk, you see, is French," Crocodile informed the Americans. "Only the sugar is native. The ice? That is American. Ice in the tropics is artificial, you see. You Americans are genius at artificial."

Getting no argument, Crocodile said: "The French brought with them an admirable culture. Saigon, they say, compares well to Paris. What did you Americans bring? Ice machines and filthy money. Your money, it becomes a god and demands worship. With all that ice and money, America must be a very cold country."

"Where is it?" asked Skinner.

"Quid pro quo," said Peckfogle.

"The product," said Skinner.

"We need to see a sample," said Peckfogle, and popped a Tums into his mouth.

"Surely a man who needs those tablets," said Crocodile, "I would recommend surgery. I have often wanted to witness a surgery. That would be quite interesting, to see how they do it, all the blood and guts exposed. I could have been a famous surgeon, if not for my leprosy. You see what it has done to my hands."

Crocodile's head swiveled and he focused on his yellow Honda, parked at the wide, open doorway. He shouted Vietnamese curses that sent street urchins and schoolboys running.

Peckfogle, wearing sandals, kicked Skinner's combat boot under the table. This to reinforce their agreement that Skinner would not bring up Crocodile's shooting of his jeep's tire.

"America is turning our youth into greedy thieves," Crocodile said. "Did you know we had a high culture before you people arrived? Poetry was our particular art. And now of course it is television. Is it any wonder I feel the urge to spit on Americans?"

Skinner and Peckfogle exchanged worried glances.

Crocodile tapped the table with stubby fingers.

"I was a child leper on the streets. An orphan. Of course they have miracle treatments now, the French brought Western doctors to our city for the first time. I admire the French. *Si vous étiez francais, j'allais accorder un crédit.*"

"Speak English," demanded Skinner.

"It means, for the French, perhaps credit. For you, money up front."

All conversation ceased as Sanny delivered ice-coffee setups for three. She had just come from school, and had not yet changed out of her Catholic uniform. It's the same all over the world: dark blazer, white blouse, dark blue skirt, white stockings. When she disappeared behind the beaded curtain, Skinner said: "We need to sample product. We're not paying five grand on faith."

"I do not wish to deal with your friend, Speck Focal. He reminds me of a scorpion. Very strongly of a scorpion. That's how I will think of your friend, Speck Focal. I will call him Specialist Scorpion."

"Do we really need this asshole, Peck?" Skinner said. "This town's full of dope dealers."

He rose from the table, walked off two steps, sat at the bar, called to Sanny for a beer. "I know you have Budweiser back there," he said, and then muttered, "little bitch."

"I raised cash with the help of this man," Peckfogle whispered to Crocodile. "He won't pay unless we're certain the product is genuine."

"Perhaps you rich Americans have ready cash, but us poor Vietnamese ... Leprosy destroys the nerves you see, and leaves us suffering with a lack of feeling."

He lifted the tiny steel pot from above his icy glass, and watched the coffee dregs pour through.

"You don't know the value of pain until you can no longer feel it. I can no longer function as a proper man, although I enjoy a good peep show. Don't you, Peck? Humiliation is quite enjoyable. Should we go to a peep show, now that we are business partners? I prefer the Perfume Club, with its much finer women."

"Fuck O Rama," muttered Skinner at the bar. "You shoot my fucking jeep again, pal..."

Crocodile did not seem to hear that. "For ten dollars," he said, "a pretty girl will fondle your penis. Don't you find that remarkable, the power of money? It leads directly to degradation, don't you think?"

He threw the stainless steel coffee pot toward his motorcycle. It hit a tire and careened into the muddy flow in the curb.

"I've been meaning to cut that dog's throat," he said, "it has pissed on my motorcycle more than once."

"We need assurance," said Peckfogle, stealing a glance at Skinner, "we need to see the product at the source, and take a sample pack. Otherwise, we are giving you money on faith. And you are not a man of faith, are you?"

"And we're going to pick the sample pack," called Skinner. "At random. At the source."

Crocodile grinned. "Very clever. Tell me why you are worried about quality?"

"We want a carton each to sell for ourselves," Skinner said, leaning toward Crocodile. "In addition to the cash."

"Once I take you to my source, it is not in Saigon by the way, then what's to stop you from shooting me and stealing it all?"

"Trust," said Skinner.

Crocodile laughed.

"Deal or no deal," muttered Skinner.

Crocodile would not speak directly to him, but turned to Peckfogle.

"Tell me Peck, why do you need to make such a profit? I hope it is not for a woman. Vietnamese women, you know, are famous for their trickery. They tell GIs they need money to help their mothers in the poor villages. And then they spend it on silk clothing and perfumes, going to American movies, drinking fancy cognac and smoking opium. Never believe one of our women. They are the very height of treachery. Do you think I would be more handsome," he paused to smile, "with white teeth?"

"Give us a carton each now," Skinner said. "We'll sell 'em on base to raise our down payment."

Crocodile laughed. "I thought you had the down payment."

"Not all of it," said Skinner.

"Tell me why," said Crocodile.

"Why what?" said Peckfogle.

"Why do you want to risk becoming a drug seller? It is a terrible occupation. Once we sold *can sa* openly in the street markets, but now, you Americans pressured our government to make a wanton crime of it. In my day, well, no rich man would hire young Crocodile, you see, with my bad eye and my awful skin and my stumpy fingers. So I had no choice. One has to make a living. Selling cigarettes and *co* is how I started the street life. But you, Peck, so young, so strong, I've heard your dick still works. And such drastic penalties the Americans seek for the simple smoking of a pleasurable puff. Tell me why you risk it."

"Because I was born to be a hero," Peckfogle said. "We all were."

Crocodile laughed.

Skinner scoffed.

Sanny delivered him a warm bottle of '33'.

"My family needs money right now," said Peckfogle. "But as soon as that's taken care of, I'm going to buy a motorcycle, and ride across the country, Staten Island to San Francisco."

"Where have I heard this before?" Skinner asked.

"Have you read Kerouac?" Peckfogle asked.

"Have I what?"

"Never mind."

"Oh, Jack Kerouac," said Crocodile. "*On the Road*, yes, yes, it is a poem about a car, no?"

"I guess you could put it that way."

"Very American. A poem about cars and money." Crocodile tapped Peckfogle on the shoulder. "Entrepreneur, is that how you say it? It's a French word, I believe. I am guessing it means destined for great wealth. In that spirit, I will sell you each a carton of my Blend for $400."

"Fuck the price," said Skinner. "We're not rubes."

"Supplies are scarce," said Crocodile. "A carton is worth $2,000 on base."

"We're not on base."

"I have spies watching the gate," Crocodile said.

"No doubt," said Skinner.

"They say Private Peckfogle passes through like magic."

"Okay," said Peckfogle. "Deal. One carton per man."

"What? At $400?" Skinner protested.

"Skinner, my mother is in a Mormon jail."

"Fuck O Rama."

"Let's get this done," said Peckfogle.

Skinner examined his warm beer, sipped and said, "Okay."

"Sanny," called Crocodile, "bring us three brandies. The French bottle, not that motor oil from America."

They passed a wordless moment as the street life rushed by in the bright sunshine beyond the doorway. Sanny set down three tiny glasses and the men hoisted and drank.

"Tomorrow at this time," Crocodile said, "a rucksack will be ready. It will contain two cartons. Sanny will direct you to it. From the time you pick it up, you have five days to deliver all my cash, plus five hundred in patience fee."

"What?" said Skinner.

"Patience fee. You'll owe me $6,000 altogether," said Crocodile. "We must move fast. Time, you see, any delay, increases risk. My source is no nonsense. He has packaged up 55 cartons, and every day he keeps them magnifies the risk. Rumors spread easily. He does not trust his own employees. The city is crawling with gangsters and thieves. His warehouse could be robbed every night. So I mean to provide you with the most sincere motivation."

He slammed his brandy glass to the table and it cracked.

"We have a deal." He wagged a finger. "No backing out now. In five days, you bring me the cash, and then we, how do you say it, consume the deal."

"Okay," said Peckfogle and drank.

"Fuck-O-Rama," said Skinner and drank.

"Peckfogle," said Crocodile, "We are all of us in danger now. Your Negro whore with the French name? She will pay with a finger for every day you are late."

CHAPTER TEN

Crocodile was wrong about many things.

On The Road was not a poem.

The women of Vietnam weren't all schemers.

Merci was Cambodian-Corsican, not African, and her occupation was bookkeeper, not whore.

Crocodile's threat to chop off Merci's fingers, I figured, was just a melodramatic warning against delay or double-cross.

Melo-dramatic.

I love that word.

The Vietnam War, it's melo-dramatic.

Starring Life vs. Death, with Dismemberment in a walk-on role.

I let Crocodile and Skinner leave the Marilyn Monroe and stepped into the back room to look for Sanny.

"Out!" she screeched.

She was changing from blue Catholic school uniform into her stained white barmaid dress.

I saw her in panties, no bra, a violation of her virgin privacy.

Yes, she was a virgin who gave $10 hand jobs. This War has produced every irony you can imagine, Your Honor.

She hissed at me and I turned around, polite and modest like a Saint Sebastian boy oughta be.

Although I did peek.

In a moment Sanny, fully dressed, bumped me from behind.

It was a friendly push. Now that I was about to become a wealthy drug dealer, she liked me.

The Blend made me popular in Vietnam, just like smut had made me a hero to the boys of Bayway.

I fired up a stub, since we both needed a magic hit of opium, tobacco, menthol, sweet dreams, toxins, cloves, marijuana and the illusion of self-importance.

Sanny smoked, oblivious, as her customers thumped the counter.

She had no motivation to work hard, since Arvin soldiers never tipped and Uncle Tin paid the same no matter how well or badly she served them.

In the deadly prosperity of war, workers were hard to find.

"I would take Merci to America if I could," I told Sanny.

I wanted to be Merci's hero. As much as I hate my father, I too am a hypocrite do-gooder. It's in the Peckfogle blood.

"Then fly with her. Jetliner, yes?"

"Red tape. It takes like months for the Army to issue a marriage license."

"You must be married?"

"You can't pack a woman into a suitcase and take her home."

"Why bother?"

"I love her," I said.

Sanny laughed. "You GIs."

"You don't believe in love?"

"Please."

"How old are you?"

"None of your bees wax, GI."

"I'll be gone soon, Sanny. One of these days I will disappear and you will hear from me never again."

"Likely story. GIs, Bien Hoa, forever. Caught like a rat in the big trap."

"Not me." I lifted the bandage and showed her my tattoo. "This is an insult to the commanders, you see?"

"No."

"When I salute, this will anger them."

"Eh, maybe you think so."

I whispered: "When they see this, they'll say: *Didi mau, Peckfogle.*"

"Merci will be sad. She likes you. She says you do not beat her."

"That's all it takes?"

"Other boyfriends, very bad."

I handed the burning stub to Sanny and said: "You're some kind of cousin to Merci, right? Aren't you all related to Mr. Tin somehow?"

Sanny exhaled smoke and snarled. "No! Wrong again, GI."

"Then you're from Merci's village, right, Sa Dec, down in the Delta?"

"No way." She blew smoke. "It's no village and I am no orphan girl, bastard of foreigners."

"Where are you from then?"

"It is my secret."

"I'm trying to help you."

"You Americans have been a great help already."

"That was sarcasm, right?"

She curled her lips as if she was sucking a lemon.

"If you're seventeen," I said, "you can marry a GI."

"I am not Marilyn Monroe, with big blond tits."

"You are very pretty."

"I am not so nice."

"You could get a GI to marry you, believe me."

"Ha! Yes, marry the GI no matter how he smells, move with him to Disneyland and file for divorce, this is a well-known trick."

"Look, I'm working a deal with your friend Crocodile ..."

"He is not my friend."

"I was being sarcastic."

"What you say?"

"I'm trying to be funny."

"No smiles in this war, Mister."

An Arvin sergeant banged an empty beer bottle on the bar and Sanny shouted: *"Không còn bia."*

"My deal with Crocodile will get Merci off the hook," I said.

"What's the hook?"

"She will no longer pay the Street Tax. That's part of the deal."

"So you do her a big favor?" Her eyes flashed. "Do me a big favor, okay?"

She whispered in my ear, warm and soft like Miss Malecki, and it gave me a boner.

"Kill Crocodile."

I looked at her, astonished.

Murder?

Hadn't she just shed the uniform of a Catholic school girl?

"You can do it, GI. He is VC spy, very bad."

"I'm a pacifist," I said.

"A what you say?"

"Give peace a chance."

"Give war a chance, you lousy coward," she said. "I have customers."

"But you're out of beer."

"Not so," she said, and ducked behind her curtain.

The Marilyn Monroe has no back door, which is dangerous, because of all the handgrenade attacks in Bien Hoa.

Hence, the sandbags stacked along the bottom of the bar, which offer at least some protection in a duck-and-cover situation.

Mr. Tin had rejected the idea of a grenade screen, since it would inhibit the flow of customers from the sidewalk tables, but this left the entire café vulnerable, and all it would take was a casual flip from a Saigon Cowboy speeding along on his putt-putt.

Mr. Tin was not worried. He spent the evenings on the roof with his pigeons. And he paid protection to Crocodile, whose "insurance policy" no doubt included a no-fragging clause.

Even so, being excessively concerned with personal safety, aka a coward, I made it a point not to linger in the dark interior of the Marilyn Monroe. It was like a cave and would only magnify the power of a grenade.

I walked outside and waited on the corner for Du Ky.

He always somehow got word I was waiting and would pick me up within minutes, so I stood in the sunny nasty heat and looked back in regret at Sanny, dodging among tables of ass-grabbing Arvins.

Sanny is darling-cute and if I was her age, I'd make a move on her.

Oh, to be a teenager again.

Wait, that was only two years ago.

This city is loaded with desperate women who'd love to take up with an American, but I don't think it's in me to betray Merci.

She's been fucked over plenty. Do I need to list the armies that have run roughshod over this beat-down nation in her short lifetime? Japanese, French, Cao Dai, Korean, Australian, Binh Xueyn, Foreign Legion, Chinese, American, Hoa Hao, North Vietnamese, Viet Minh, Viet Cong. Maybe the Japanese were the worst. Merci was born during the "Japanese famine," when Delta rice was diverted to feed Hirohito's troops, while the locals starved.

After a childhood too terrible to remember, she's cold to me and that's how I know she's desperate for love. She's afraid of love and the more you fight love, the more you need it.

Merci ended her childhood in a Catholic orphanage after her worthless father was killed at Dien Bien Phu and her mother died of some horrible tropical infection.

A famous nun passed while I was waiting for Du Ky in the shade of the movie theater's doorway.

Well, she was famous around here, anyway.

Her name was Sister Helena, and she was seen every day on the Avenue of Whores, an older European, walking eyes raised toward heaven, past bars, opium dens, massage parlors and bordellos.

She wore not a habit but white skirt and blouse, a dark blue kerchief around her short-cut hair, and a wooden cross dangling at her breast. In a back alley across from the city park, she ran a clinic that tended to the needs of sick prostitutes.

Thirteen years of Catholic school, and I had never met a nun who glowed like she did, with compassion and dignity. I suppose a saint wouldn't have wasted her time, anyway, on such miscreants as attended Saint Sebastian's.

Neither had Merci ever experienced a loving nun. We'd swapped nun horror stories, hers being worse than mine by a factor of a thousand. She has Third World scars, on shoulders and buttocks, while my nun scars are only First World, humiliation.

I had met Merci at the STEAM BATH MASSAGE when she was the manager and I, what the hell, I admit it, was a frequent customer.

One day when all the steam room girls were occupied, I assumed she was the Madam and would provide last-resort massage services, given that this was payday and very busy.

She snarled.

"You are a fool to think I do dirty things. I am a professional."

I backed away. She was drinking a Coke, smoking a long elegant Basto cigarette and reading a fashion magazine.

"Sorry," I said.

"How much?" she asked.

"Double," I said.

She sputtered. "Not for a hundred."

"I don't have that much anyway."

"I hate GIs. Only trouble."

"Not all of us are bad."

"So you say!"

She stubbed out a cigarette. I noticed her red fingernails.

How many times had they coaxed $10 out of a GI's cock?

But it turns out, that was an unwarranted assumption.

"I am a strict Catholic," she said.

I fell in love right there.

True, she was over thirty and I was shy of twenty-one.

True, she had a face full of pock marks and a twisted lip.

True, most Vietnamese girls, like Sanny, were as willowy as runway models, while Merci was built like a truck.

I didn't care. A damaged, bitter Catholic, just my type.

"Strict? How strict?"

"You cannot believe."

"Try me."

"I was forced to serve Mass. No boys! We girls had okay from the Bishop of Vinh Long, but I hear that in America you must have a swinging dick to serve Mass."

"Swinging dick?"

"Like you GIs say."

"Then you were an altar girl."

"*Mea culpa, mea culpa, mea maxima ...*"

I said: "Oh ... My ... God."

She tapped her head. "I have the Latin Mass in my head, forever."

"Can I take you out for a glass of sacramental wine?"

"Is this a joke?"

"Yes, a serious joke. I'd like to take you out."

"What does this mean in America, take you out."

"It means..."

"I'm warning you, GI, I have seen all your movies." She formed her fist into a gun. "It means gangster-kill me."

"No, that's *rub you out.* I want to *take* you out. Boyfriend, *bạn trai.*"

"Boyfriend? Troi oi!"

"You already have one?"

"No thank you because I am always working and I do not drink alcohol and I am not seen in American whore bars ever. My mother was Cao Dai you know, and they are even more strict than Catholics, as they are watched every moment by the eye of God, and she would be red-faced with shame to have mothered a drunken slut."

"How about we just go get a bowl of pho?"

She curled her lips as if disgusted. "Perhaps you could bring me soup from across the street, it is quite the good stuff, but I cannot leave my desk or they will rob me blind."

"The girls?"

"No, the evil GIs." She sighed. "In my next life, I will be a designer of fancy gowns. What do you think?"

"I'm hungry for pho."

"I will have the shaved beef if you are feeling generous as it is the most expensive, but do not allow them to put in the hot peppers as I like to do that myself."

So I dashed across the street to the soup shop, dodging a ragged shoeshine boy who kept shouting "GI ... shine ... GI."

Fifty-fifty chance he was a runt informant for the VC.

The pho shop was a humble affair balanced on a raw wood counter, a three-pot, mother-daughter operation. The young men in this nation were either dead or in uniform, and commerce had turned decidedly feminine.

I ordered beef for Merci and vegetarian for myself, although I strongly suspect they used chicken broth in the vegetarian.

There was a surplus of dead chickens in Bien Hoa.

There was a surplus of dead everything in Bien Hoa.

As Mama-san ladled soup I composed in my head a marriage proposal to Merci.

I had me the perfect woman.

I imagined bringing her home to New Jersey in triumph and converting her to a meatless existence.

My free-thinker mom, long since sprung from jail, would welcome my choice, even if it was a chubby foreign woman with crooked teeth. But my father, the great faux humanist "Adam" Peckfogle, he would go off like a moon-shot rocket.

What! An Oriental whore?

He's not the Adam Peckfogle you might have read about in the Newark Star Ledger.

He's never cared about animals, despite all the publicity.

Exhibit A: When I was nine years old, he took my dog Skippy "out to Uncle T.J.'s farm" because Skippy had crapped on the dining room carpet.

But I give the asshole credit, he knew a great scam when he stumbled upon it.

As president of the Blessed Saviors of Animals Foundation, he sets his own salary and spends winters at Hallendale, Florida and summers at Saratoga, New York.

Both those towns just happen to have famous race tracks.

He claims he attends Saratoga every season to monitor the treatment of the thoroughbreds. If you believe that one, I've got a lame race horse to sell you.

Yes, my father, stage name Adam Peckfogle, is CEO of Blessed Saviors of Animals.

He is also a degenerate horse player.

Who used a jockey's whip to discipline his children.

I loved to imagine the moment I introduced him to Merci. She's a tough, honest person who's made a living by her wits in the world's most dangerous city.

He's a phony who sold the family farm, gambled the money away, then recovered by scamming naïve animal-lovers.

The minute he saw Merci, he'd scream that venereal disease had gone to my brain. He'd threaten to commit me to a mental institution and then rant about how the fire at Saint Sebastian's had disgraced the Peckfogle name. He'd claim I was living my life so as to deliberately embarrass him in public.

His foundation's sneaky lawyers would try to get Merci deported, or failing that, have our marriage annulled. He'd wag his finger and vow that he'd never tolerate a Japanese grandson, didn't I know what they had done to us at Pearl Harbor, the sneaky slant-eyed bastards?

It would do no good to point out that Merci wasn't even vaguely Japanese. That Merci and her mother were nearly starved to death by the Japanese.

That's why Merci's fat today, Your Honor. She eats hearty. Her childhood was a desperate scramble for food.

"No pepper, no no no," I said to the soup mama-san.

But it wasn't just to piss off the Great Humanist that I fantasized about marrying Merci.

I'm a selfish guy like any other and I was thinking of all Merci could do for me.

For her, America would be a *tabula raza*, as the philosophers say.

I imagined her tagging along when I did a Jack Kerouac, put her on the back of a motorcycle, dipped its back wheel into the filthy Arthur Kill, bid New Jersey goodbye forever, and headed for the pure blue Pacific.

Nor would she protest when she discovered my ambition to become a San Francisco beatnik poet.

I figured poetry was just the next logical step, and my experience as a Government Fiction Writer might get me into the poetry program at San Francisco State, if indeed they even had one.

While I was busy writing award-wining poetry, Merci, industrious soul that she is, would find plenty of opportunity in the Land of Lucre.

Would any American girl work to support a beatnik-poet?

A refugee bookkeeper married to a Lapsed Catholic poet, what could be better?

I crossed the street balancing two ceramic bowls of pho, laid them on the STEAM BATH counter and announced: "We should get married."

Merci approached the counter, gave a skeptical look into the soup bowl and said: "Spoon? Chopsticks?"

"I figured you had some..."

"This is no shitty cafe ... " her eyes shifted to take in my nametag "Corporal Peck-Vo-Gull"

Yes, I had attained the august rank of Corporal back in my halcyon days. Getting that second stripe was the highpoint of my military career.

Which is not saying a heck of a lot.

"I'll be right back with spoons and chopsticks," I said.

"You are handsome," she said.

"You think so?"

"But you are just a boy. Even though I will look like your mother-in-law, perhaps I will marry you when I give up on my dreams. Why not? We will see."

On that optimistic note, I left her. I was standing in the shade of the movie theater doorway, lost in remembering the recent past and imagining the blissful and poetic future.

Du Ky puttered up in his dirty rickshaw and shattered my dream-state.

"You have smoke for me?" he asked.

"Not today," I said. "Maybe tomorrow."

CHAPTER ELEVEN

The Graves Registration shower hut stood across a muddy lane, just behind the big pile of coffins. It was a wooden shanty with a concrete floor and a black steel water tank on the roof. Fifty-fifty chance there was actually water in the tank.

The tank was refilled by a water truck, as there was no piping at this neglected end of the base. Location, location, location, they say, and the morgue and its neighbor, the ammo dump, was not the most attractive real estate in town.

I liked to shower just after dawn, alone, when the water was coolest and the other GIs were pigging out on bacon, ham and sausage at the mess hall.

When my rubber shower clogs hit the wet cement, Miss Hanh looked up, startled. But when she saw it was only me, she half-smiled, and turned her back. She was working in the corner, scrubbing laundry in a tub.

Miss Hanh was the youngest hooch maid in the quad, which meant she was constantly harassed by horny soldiers. She seemed like the shyest girl I'd ever met.

She did her housekeeping job quietly, shining boots, making beds, and sweeping up the barracks. The laundry was her side-gig. GIs got their clothes cleaned free, at the huge Vietnamese-run laundry on base, but the uniforms came back stiff with starch, so most soldiers paid a hoochmaid to do a softer wash.

The shower room had the only water in the area, and Miss Hahn was forced to use it for her mini-business.

I had seen some nasty scenarios in this shower, with guys holding their dicks and prancing before Miss Hanh. I recognized her as a fellow victim of Army oppression. Nudity was no big deal in Vietnam. In the villages, young people would just shed their clothes and jump in the nearest river for relief from the heat. So I quietly slipped out of my clothes and showered on the far side of the room, seven shower heads away from the shy laundress.

I let the cool water flow, opened my plastic soap case, and lathered up. I closed my eyes against the sting when the soapy water ran over my face. When I rinsed and opened my eyes again, I saw a nightmare two shower heads over.

Colonel Carl Sadler, commander of the MPs.

Nude.

Sadler was a long, lean muscular son of a bitch, baldish gray on top. He had the penis of a draft animal.

Miss Hanh scurried out of the laundry room, lugging her tub full of olive-drab uniforms.

"Private Peckfogle," said the colonel.

"Yes, sir."

The colonel did a slow pirouette under the dripping shower head.

"Do you know what I would like, private?"

"No sir."

"I would like to facilitate your exit from my beloved Army." He sputtered, as if his mouth had taken in soap.

"Well…" I said, but my mind failed to find the right gear. I kept my right hand, with its FTA tattoo, hidden from the colonel.

"Conscription was a tragic error," the colonel said. "War and democracy don't mix. And so it has come to this: A million men with no military aptitude blundering through two years of obligatory service, rather than nobly serving their nation. "

"You could put it that way, sir."

"I just did. Do you realize, private, the severity of the drug problem on our base?"

He turned off the water and rubbed his head with an olive drab towel. Then he draped it around his shoulders. Its corners were emblazoned with his rank, the Full Bird, the gold, spread-winged eagle.

"I don't have any personal knowledge of drug use, sir," I said.

My voice sounded squeaky, even to me.

"Of course not," said the colonel, and cleared his throat. "But I look over my command and I see drug dogs, pat-downs, long lines at Main Gate. It's a security issue to have men in a cluster-fuck outside the gate, waiting to be checked for drugs. A VC machine gunner driving by, that's the stuff of my nightmares. There would be an inquest, and my boys would take the blame. This is not the way I want to run my command. We're an Army, not a drug rehab clinic, and we've got a war to win here."

Water dribbling down my face, I nodded. I began to have dark sweaty visions of another term in LBJ.

"Private Peckfogle, salute me."

"My hand is injured, sir."

"That's an order, private."

"Sir, may I…"

"Now!"

I saluted, trying to slant FTA away from the colonel's view.

The colonel did not return my salute.

"Nothing personal, sir," I said.

"Just as I'd heard," said the colonel.

I held my salute.

"Not much happens on this base that doesn't get back to me," Colonel Sadler said. "At ease, private."

I dropped my right hand to my side.

"I do not care to court martial you for insubordination. You're not to blame for the misbegotten policy of conscription. You were never meant to be a soldier. Did Alexander the Great have draftees? I'll answer that question for you. His fighters were all volunteers. Julius Caesar? Same answer. The great Armies of history were composed of willing soldiers not … foot-dragging hippies. Peckfogle, have you encountered Jesus as your personal savior?"

"I'm not devout, sir. Religion was thrust upon me sir, as was military service."

"I thought so. Do you wish to be honorably discharged?"

"Yes sir, I do. Soon and sincerely."

"An honorable discharge would come with a lifetime of benefits, including the GI Bill, and in your case, mental health services."

"I'm aware of that sir."

"Four years in college. Imagine yourself on campus, impressing hairy-legged hippie girls with your made-up war stories."

"Sounds good, sir."

"Captain Clark reports that you're a misguided man, but not an evil one. He says you're sincere in your anti-authoritarian beliefs, and that they are deeply rooted in your warped personality."

I shrugged.

"I am about to grant you dark authority to buy drugs, private. Your mission will be to work undercover. You will identify the traitor or traitors behind the import of drugs to my base. I'll expect you to begin providing names to me in a week's time."

"Me?"

"That tattoo, Peckfogle, has already made you notorious. Are you not aware of how quickly rumors spread during wartime? If you aren't already, you will soon be known all over Long Binh to be in the bad graces of this command. You'll be notorious, and therefore, the perfect undercover agent."

"An agent?"

"Your parole officer, Brennan, will be your monitor."

The colonel stepped into olive-drab boxer shorts. "When your mission is accomplished, it will be announced that you have pled guilty to insubordination for the crime of obtaining that tattoo. You will be, as far as anyone here knows, shipped in handcuffs to Leavenworth to begin your sentence. But that will only be a cover story. In actuality you will be honorably discharged at the Oakland Army Terminal. You will enjoy the traditional steak dinner ...

"I'm a vegetarian, sir."

"Mashed potatoes then. Whatever your civilian destiny, you will be free to pursue it upon honorable discharge."

"An undercover agent?" I asked. "Me? Are you joking, colonel?"

The colonel buttoned his starched tunic over his gray-haired, muscular chest. "War is not a joke, son."

CHAPTER TWELVE

Deep inside the Dead Letter Bunker, I banged away on my Underwood.

Even on the brightest morning, no light leaked in, just as no light has leaked into my dark soul since I was sworn in to the Army. Electric power was on the blink so I wrote by the light of a mil-spec Coleman lantern.

Dear Mom:

I was sorry to hear from you-know-who that you'd been arrested. How are they treating you?

I will try to call from the outside, but the phone system's dicey in town and there's no phone service on base unless you are high-ranking brass. I hope that by the time this letter reaches the U.S., Dolly or Benjamin will have helped to free you.

Sorry to say, I have lost touch with both of them.

I feel powerless to help you from so far away. I hold you in my heart always as the good person who kept our family together at great personal cost. I will not forget you or abandon you.

I am working with my commanders on a compassion discharge and with luck, could be back in the States by next week.

Otherwise, I am in the black hole of communications here, and am powerless to do anything but write letters. It will be a slow and awkward process to negotiate with an Idaho attorney at this distance, but that is my Plan B if my discharge is delayed.

I'm coming for you, mom, and I'm going to get you out.

You may be worried about me, because of the war and all, but don't. I am the safest man in Vietnam, living in a bunker and doing clerical chores. The most dangerous thing I do all day is take a can opener to my C-rations.

Love you to pieces, mom.

I will be there. Soon!

Your devoted son

JJ

As I ripped that letter out of the typewriter, I remembered having a smelly dream.

It was the dream of a honey-wagon, idling at the Main Gate.

Just idling and emitting awful shit fumes.

Who dreams in smells?

Somebody who smokes too much Blend.

I wondered about that dream as I folded my letter to Mom and stuffed it into an olive-drab envelope. Then I rolled a sheet of cheap yellow teletype paper into the Underwood and typed out my plan in bullet points.

- SNEAK two cartons of the Blend onto the base.
- SELL them on payday.
- USE the profit to finance Crocodile's big deal.
- ARRANGE for Skinner's diversionary firefight.
- SMUGGLE Crocodile's 55 cartons in a duffel bag.
- DELIVER it to Crocodile's "inside man" whoever that was
- BETRAY the "inside man" to Colonel Sadler

• GIVE Merci bribe money for a visa.
• FLY to America
• GET Mom out of prison.

I ripped that list out of the typewriter.

How did that stinky honey wagon dream fit in?

Satisfied with my list, I burned it in an ashtray, but then had a worrisome thought: If this was going to work, the "inside man" would have to pay Crocodile *before* the Colonel's MPs closed in.

Sister Charles would call that a complex sentence.

I would call that a frightening sentence.

My plan to rescue both Merci and Mom only had a chance if Crocodile got his money.

Any glitch in the timing or the payout, and the whole thing would crash and burn. If Sadler's goons were tailing me, and closed in before all the money changed hands, Merci would never escape Cong Ly Street and my mom would be sentenced to a year studying the Book of Mormon.

I dressed in my best clean fatigue shirt, with the shadows where my corporal stripes had been removed, then worked into ragged blue-jean cut-off shorts.

Me a spy? I'm not sure I was cut out for this James Bond crap, being neither suave nor British.

I stepped out of my dark cavern into brutal blinding sunlight, crossed the muddy alley and opened the creaky wooden door to the shower room.

Miss Hanh was scrubbing camouflage uniforms in a galvanized tub, squatting in purple blouse, black pajamas, conical hat with purple ribbon, rough bar of Cascade soap in hand, her bare feet splayed on the wet concrete floor.

Miss Hanh, who had learned never to look up.

I sat on a moldy wood bench across from her.

Scrub scrub with a stiff brush.

"Miss Hanh?"

"Good morning."

"Miss Hanh, would you smoke with me?"

I removed from my top pocket a rumpled package of Kools. Only one cigarette was left, a twisted thing that looked as if it had been stepped on.

Miss Hanh smiled.

It was a crooked Kool, so it was The Blend. The Vietnamese called these cigarettes *mơ tưởng, or* "The Dream."

She said something in Vietnamese that I did not understand, followed by: "I am happy."

Miss Hanh dropped her brush into her laundry bucket and stood up, drying her hands on her blouse. Even in a land of skinny women, Miss Hanh was remarkably thin, and might have weighed shy of 80 pounds.

I patted the bench and she sat next to me. For a tiny woman she had giant bare feet.

Rice paddy feet.

Using a C-ration waterproof match, I fired the limp cigarette, inhaled, held and coughed smoke.

I passed the cigarette to Miss Hanh.

She closed her eyes and inhaled.

"Never say love," she said.

What? Had I heard that right?

"Never say love," said Miss Hanh, "if you don't mean it."

"What the heck are you talking about?"

"Americans say so. It's the Love Story. I have seen it..." she held up four fingers... "beau coup times."

She passed the cigarette back and sighed. "Matinee," she said.

She rested a hand on my bare thigh. "I like you," she said. "You are handsome like Mister Ryan O'Neal."

The Blend did that.

Hallucinations.

With the Blend you often saw what you feared or desired, which, often enough, was the same thing.

I inhaled and sat back, getting a warm one under the influence of Miss Hahn's touch. Vietnam had taken a lot of the manhood out of me, but now sitting beside this cute laundress, it was like Miss Malecki all over again.

Oh, the blond Polish dreamboat Miss Malecki.

When Miss Hanh lifted her hand to take the cigarette, a chill disappointment washed over me. Women have such power over horny boys.

"Finished," said Miss Hanh. "I work very hard."

She burned herself taking in the last puff, dropped the ember, and then sucked her burned fingers.

She removed her conical hat and set it in her lap. Her black hair, shiny clean and held in a bun, would have reached her waist if unleashed.

"You have girlfriend?" she asked.

"Ah ..." I lied.

"I can be," said Miss Hanh. "Maybe. You are the good GI."

"I'm going home soon."

"Too bad," said Miss Hanh. "Love means you are never sorry."

"That's a line from the movie, right?"

"Ha."

"What do you mean, ha?"

"Ha."

"Miss Hanh, how long have you been working here?"

She seemed not to understand.

"How many years, Long Binh? Years, you *bic?*"

She held up three fingers.

"Three years?" Peckfogle said.

"Beau coup years."

"Then you must know a lot of Viet people on this base."

She shrugged her skinny shoulders. "Ti-ti."

"Do you know anyone who drives a honey wagon?"

I was ready to explain that question but Miss Hanh nodded. "Of course."

"What do you mean, of course?"

"It is good nature."

How much was she understanding?

"Drive," I said, and pantomimed turning a steering wheel. "You *bic* drive, honey wagon?"

"Yes, I told you, mister, yes."

"Who do you know?"

"Mr. Phan. Driving."

"When does he come through the gate? Every day?"

"Every one day."

"Once a day?"

She held up two fingers. "Beau coup."

"I want to meet him."

"For sure. He is handsome. Like you."

She held her nose.

"But he smells."

"Today. I want to meet him today."

"Okay. You have more *mơ tưởng* cigarettes?"

"After I meet him, beau coup *mơ tưởng* cigarettes."

I stood and kissed the top of her fragrant beautiful hair.

"I like you, Miss Hanh."

"Love is so sorry, mister."

CHAPTER THIRTEEN

"Okay, Skinner, man, I've got it now."

Skinner and I were walking the wire, his Sector, 23.

Needless to say it was hot.

But I'm saying it anyway.

I walked gingerly in a world of sweat, land mines and concertina wire.

The base was surrounded by seven layers of concertina, and then a regular barbed-wire fence in front of that curlicue mess. At the base of each fence post, a gray Claymore mine was set on little feet, a curved gray brick in the sand.

Who was this Claymore guy, anyway?

Did he go home and tell the wife and kiddies: You know what Daddy did at work today? He invented a pack of BBs that explodes and rips people to shreds.

Wow, Daddy, tell us more.

And when the Claymore kiddies go to school, the nun asks: What does your Daddy do, Johnny Claymore?

He makes landmines, Sister. They can kill a hundred people in a flash.

Johnny Claymore, you must be so proud.

Skinner knelt in the weedy sand to turn a Claymore around so that the words FRONT TOWARD ENEMY faced away from his tower.

"Sneaky fuckers," said Skinner, "they crawl in at night and reverse the Claymores.

He was sweating down the stubble of his always-red face.

"Right under your nose," Skinner said. "Nothing works. Searchlights, dogs, your basic Commie is a sneaky Commie."

He rose and wiggled the barbed wire, rattling the beer cans that had been hung along it, beer cans that jangled in the slightest breeze but were oddly silent when the wire was breeched by VC sappers.

"Don't you sweat, Peckfogle?"

"I am sweating."

"Not in rivers like I am."

"The key is to avoid work."

"Well," Skinner wiped his face with his forearm, "if I avoid this work, I end up with a head full of BBs." He sighed. "Vicious fuckers."

"Skinner, what if the Chinese invaded Illinois?"

"They don't have the balls."

"Wouldn't you fight back? Wouldn't you sneak up on their bases and turn their landmines around?"

"Fuck no. I'm not a fucking dink. I fight man to man. Your point?"

"Obvious isn't it?"

"The Chinese don't have the balls to invade America. Period."

I followed him along a narrow treacherous path out of the maze of barbed wire and into the somewhat less sweltering shade underneath a tower built of railroad ties.

Even those railroad ties were sweating, oozing black goo.

"I'll get our cartons through."

"How?" said Skinner, his red bearded face dripping sweat.

"Honey wagon."

"Stupid. You'll get caught. They search those trucks."

"Not every time."

"The MPs are way ahead of you, man. The dogs can pick it out. Maybe a GI can't tell shit from Shinola, but those dogs can."

"I will distract the dog handlers. You know Freckles, the MP? He's one of the good ones."

Skinner inclined his head, like he was trying to find an angle that would admit a thought.

"Peckfogle, when they drag you off to LBJ, I don't know you. You're the bereavement box guy, come into the PO once a day, that's all I know."

I swept my eyes along the weedy swampy horizon.

I imagined an NVA division, stumbling through the muck.

Led by Sister Charles in black habit, wielding a ruler.

And John Adams Peckfogle holding a jockey's whip.

The Blend does that to you sometimes.

"Got the cash?" I asked.

"Working on it," Skinner said. "Mom's sending a Postal Money Order."

He kicked the sand between his combat boots. "Fucking scorpions," he said. "God, I hate this country."

"When's your money coming?" I asked.

"Maybe tonight," he said. "Even when I cash Mom's check, I'm a little short."

"How much?"

"But I'm the mail guy, right?"

"What does that mean?"

"Guys send cash home, right, to moms and sweethearts?"

"Yeah?"

"They shouldn't send cash, we tell them all the time, but they do it." He belched. "Not all that cash makes it home, all's I'm saying."

"You wouldn't do that, Skinner."

"You can definitely feel the cash in the envelopes. Fuck O Rama, it's been done before."

"How much are you short?"

"Seven twenty five."

I whistled. No big deal in America, maybe, but over here, four months pay. I could feel myself slip-sliding. I envisioned Sister Charles, in black habit, standing next to me, measuring me with her yardstick, and I was coming up short.

Which meant I was two feet tall.

Morally.

"You want to make this deal or no?" said Skinner. "Fuck O Rama, man, I can't snap my fingers and make cash appear."

"Apparently you can conjure cash out of the mail."

"Your mom's in a Mormon jail."

"Yeah."

"So," he shrugged. "Mormons are worse than dinks. We drove 'em out of Illinois."

"Who?"

"The Mormons."

"I thought you didn't know much about history?"

"This ain't history, its family legends, all's we're talking. We drove everybody out of Illinois. Blacks,

Jews, Mormons, Catholics, all of 'em. Mormons belong in Utah, drinking salty lake water, all's I'm saying."

"And Catholics?"

"Keep 'em in Chicago with the Spades."

He sighed and gazed at the hazy horizon.

What did he see there in his Blended vision? Rows of corn, knee high by the 4th of July? Horse-drawn plows? Shotguns? Burning crosses? Blood splashed on synagogues? Terrified Mormon families on the run?

"So," he said, "I divert a little cash."

"I don't know."

"The moms and girlfriends would approve if they knew where the cash was going, excellent cause."

"Won't they trace the missing mail back to you?"

"One day burst, nah. You know how it is. Nobody really cares. Just say fuck it and drive on."

A jeep rolled by, slowly, a guy at the wheel whose uniform had a rank but no other insignia. He was W2 Thomas Brennan, aka my parole officer and minder. Colonel Sadler had our base on a drug lockdown, his MPs circling the perimeter, while his Criminal Investigations Division sent snoops like Brennan all over the base.

"If you're going to do it, save the envelopes." I whispered that, although Brennan was already driving away.

"What?"

"If you rip off the mail, save the envelopes. We'll just be borrowing the money. It'll get to the girls and moms a few days late, that's all."

"We don't save the envelopes, they're evidence, asshole. Didn't you just see a CID narc drive by and stare at us?"

"We can't just steal their money, Skinner."

He shook his head. "Catholic school," he said, "done stupid to your brain."

I felt like a mad scientist, putting together the magic formula, one ingredient at a time.

Next was Mr. Phan.

Neither Merci nor Sanny nor Du Ky nor Crocodile knew him, and I couldn't communicate very well with Miss Hanh, so I was forced to ambush him.

I stalked the main traffic circle and after a few tries, found a QC who understood at least a few words of English.

These QCs were military police for the South Vietnamese Army, but they weren't much more than traffic cops.

The GIs laughed at QCs, and called them Queer Cops.

I paid this one a $20 bribe, which for him was a week's pay. He looked like a teenager and stood about five feet tall. He wore a black helmet emblazoned with the white initials QC, and from his belt hung a pistol, a nightstick and a handcuffs case.

I hailed him in the sticky-melting asphalt of a Shell gas station and we stood there a while in the heat, me hoping he understood what I wanted.

We waited for almost an hour, during which time the QC hit me up for an orange soda and a pack of Salems.

We waited while inhaling the exhaust of military trucks, cyclos, jeeps, mini-buses, rickshaws, and God help us all, French-built autos.

When Mr. Phan's truck finally came lumbering, leaking and stinking around the circle, I frantically waved my arms. The QC raised a steel stop sign.

The truck stopped, squeaking on bad brakes, with cyclos and mini-buses whizzing around it, and I hopped up on the running board, gagging.

The truck was leaking shit-water into the street.

How could even a dog's nose parse drugs through the filthy waves of GI shit stench?

The QC refused to approach the truck with me.

There went any hope of translation.

Hoping Mr. Phan could speak English, and quickly, I gagged down a pulse of vomit and shouted: "You bring for me, okay?"

Young Mr. Phan, with gold teeth that reminded me of Crocodile, grinned and nodded.

"Cigarettes," I said. "Through gate. Okay?"

Mr. Phan, bare-chested, nodded.

I noticed a silver cross dangling against his skinny chest.

A Catholic!

Great.

He would understand corruption.

"Beaucoup dollars, okay?"

Mr. Phan waved his hand in front of his nose, as if I were the one who stank.

"I pay you, yes?" I shouted, and dug from my pocket the opening gambit, a $5 bill.

I might as well have showed him a hand grenade.

He put the truck into gear and clanked off, me clinging to the running board.

"Miss Hahn," I shouted. "She's my friend. You. Me. Miss Hahn."

And then I had to jump off, stumble into the roadside dust, and watch the honey wagon drive away. I arose to see the QC drinking orange soda, smoking a Salem, and laughing at me.

"What just happened?" I asked.

"Maybe," said the QC, "he thinks you're a sweet boy."

"A what?"

He made the universal finger-and-fist gesture for sexual intercourse.

"Maybe boys like boys."

So Mr. Phan, shit truck driver, had thought I was propositioning him.

Well, actually, it *was* a proposition, but not the kind he thought.

So, my plan was delayed for a day, another day of brutal heat, trying to keep off thoughts of my devout rosary-praying Irish-Catholic mother, being tormented by the Angel Moroni.

I hustled out the Main Gate, but among the hundred or so cyclo drivers waiting to give a GI a ride, I saw no Du Ky.

So I picked the pathetic old man who looked most desperate for a fare, hopped in back, and he took off putt putt putt.

No words were necessary since there were only two end points in this transit system: Main Gate and the Avenue of Whores.

Away we rode into the hot air, the something's-burning-stink, the perfume scent of tropical flowers, the rot stench of long-standing water, all of it rushing up the olfactory at 60 kilometers per.

It reminded me of summer days, when I rode my Triumph Bonneville over the Goethals Bridge and parked it in front of Mombo Bill's.

Nobody ever did the Mombo at Mombo Bill's, nor was the proprietor named Bill.

The joint was run by a thick-set lady of about 60 very hard years, with gray curly hair, gray eyes, and snarling lips. She kept a double-barreled, sawed-off shotgun behind the bar.

One barrel was for the Able Seamen of Mariner's Harbor and the other for the Catholic school kids from Bayway.

The Seamen drank shots-and-beers. We Bayway Boys drank 7 and 7s, and our scruffy girlfriends quaffed liquid candy, aka sloe gin fizzes.

The kids couldn't legally drink on the Jersey side of the Arthur Kill until they were 21, but in New York the legal age was 18, and at joints like Mombo Bill's, a fake driver's license had turned many a 16-year-old into a drunk.

As far as a I know, despite the obvious violations, including children throwing up on the streets, the Staten Island police never raided Mombo Bill's.

Speaking of Mombo Bill's, I made a date with Miss Malecki for the Saturday night of graduation.

Actually it wasn't really a date but I did leave a note in her pigeon hole on the last day of class.

Dear Miss Malecki, it said, *I love you, meet me at Mombo Bill's on Staten Island after the graduation ceremonies, I'll be waiting for you, we'll drink a sloe-gin fizz and go for a ride on my motorcycle.*

Did she show?

Only a horny boy could possibly have thought that would work.

That was the night that I, disappointed in love, and fueled by Mombo Bill's cheap booze, rode my Triumph back over the bridge to Bayway and lit really a lot of candles at Saint Sebastians.

I regret it now.

But it was not arson, like the cops said.

It was flames of devotion.

To Miss Malecki.

I wonder about her now as I sit in a thumping weaving motorized rickshaw on a highway where any passing motorcyclist might drop a grenade in your lap.

Turning down the muddy Cong Ly Street, aka the Avenue of Whores, it all came into view. My home away from home. Yellow and red flags of the Republic hanging outside the shops, electric wires dangling dangerously overhead, bicycles, cyclos and jeeps crossing every which way, hungry stray dogs, merchant ladies carrying baskets, the pharmacy, the swarming shoeshine boys, the tobacco shop, the canned-goods grocery, and there I am, dismounting the cyclo under the banner for the movie LOVE STORY with RYAN O'NEAL.

Just underneath that banner, a white-clad nun was tending to an old sick ragged man who squatted at the mouth of a dirty alley. Sister Helena, yes of course, that was her. I stifled the Catholic schoolboy impulse to greet her with a fake-cheerful *Good Afternoon, Sister.* I walked around the corner to where Du Ky might be found, at his friend Kinh's gas station.

It wasn't a gas station like you'd find back in the world, all white tiles with almost clean restrooms and owned by Texaco.

It was a filthy, leaky, highly flammable 55 gallon drum with hand pump attached, dispensing liters to the cyclo drivers. Like his gasoline barrel, the cockeyed Kinh was round and greasy.

I suspected he and Du Ky were ahem more than friends, but I pretended not to notice. Vietnamese men hold hands with their buddies, whether straight or gay, so you never know.

Kinh's only customers were Vietnamese, and he had no need for English.

"*O dau Du Ky?*"

Rather than answer, he tipped his hand before his lips in the gesture that, in any language, means *drinking.*

I walked around the block and was surprised to find Du Ky at the Marilyn Monroe, alone at the bar with a glass of dark liquor.

Usually he didn't drink more than half a beer. Café life was expensive and he was poor, and besides, he preferred The Blend.

I gave him a light slap on the back and said, "This is no way to make money, my friend."

"My man Peck," he said.

"Drunk already?"

"Yes. I am easy."

I sniffed his drink.

"Cognac?"

"Yes."

"Sanny?" I called. "Cognac, *s'il vous plait.*"

"I am goodbye to this world."

"What are you talking about?"

Dirty glass to his lips he said: "I am death."

"What do you mean?"

"End of the line. Last Picture Show."

Sanny set a cognac in front of me and I threw her a quizzical look. She shrugged and disappeared behind her beaded curtain, whick whick.

"Did you get some bad news, Du Ky?"

"Lousy," he said and swallowed liquor.

"Have you been at the doctor's?"

"It is too late for me, Peckfogle. Say goodbye."

He stuck out his dirty crusty hand. "Shake hands, John Wayne. Say goodbye, partner."

I looked around, saw nobody menacing, just a few Arvins playing cards and drinking warm beer at the tables.

Marilyn Monroe peered down on me from a black and white publicity photo. I could swear she winked like Miss Malecki used to, a wink that said: *You're a bad boy Jay Peckfogle and I'm sweet on you.*

"Is Crocodile after you?" I asked.

Du Ky pursed his lips. "I have no son, Peckfogle, I am a loser disgrace. Empty."

I saw Sanny spying on us from behind the bead curtain.

"What's wrong with him?" I demanded of Sanny.

She circled her ear with one finger. *"Dinky dau."*

"The first nine day period," said Du Ky. "Most important."

"What are you talking about?"

"He is Cao Dai," said Sanny from behind the curtain. "They pray for the dead nine days."

"But he is not dead."

"Doomed," yelled Sanny. "Bad card."

Suddenly, I understood. "This is all about a tarot reading?"

"She has never been wrong, Ba Gi," Sanny said.

"What was her prediction?"

"The Supreme One is lonely, and wants another soul."

"Nonsense," I said. I drained my cognac. "Come on Du Ky, we're getting out of here. I need a ride."

We stepped out into the humid sunshine.

Du Ky always wore two hats, a floppy one underneath a pith helmet.

The helmet was supposed to protect him against falls from his cyclo, although it had no strap and would fly off in a crash. It was more a good luck totem than anything. He flung the helmet into the dark cave of the Marilyn Monroe.

"I am ready," he said. "We ride."

"No helmet?"

"I am son of blood, father of death."

"I actually don't need a ride. I need translation services."

"How much?"

"If you're a dead man, what do you care?"

"My mother is not well."

"Ten bucks for the translation," I said. "Plus a dollar each way for the ride."

"Greenbacks?"

"Yes, and a couple of smokes."

"You're a good man."

"I'm a moral midget."

"A what?"

"Let's ride. It's going to be a stinky job."

"After I'm gone," he said, "you will find a good driver. I know many boys, I'll fix you up, you'll see."

"Ba Gi is just an old fortune-telling grandma looking to make a few piasters," I said. "Don't take her seriously."

"Dollars, please!" he said. "Piasters? No good."

"Tomorrow, buddy. Translate for me. Tomorrow we make beaucoup dollars."

CHAPTER FOURTEEN

My new role as drug spy rattled me, so naturally, I had to smoke The Blend to calm down.

I was in bed with Merci on a cloudy, stinky, humid afternoon.

We were damp.

Our personal dew point hovered between 99 and 100.

I was performing a slow massage of her breasts underneath her T-shirt while she puffed a Basto and blew the smoke into the slipstream of the greasy black Westinghouse fan.

She managed a massage parlor, but had never given a massage, or gotten one, until now.

Or so she said.

"I like when you sometime fuck me," she said, "but not now, please, it is too hot for love."

"Love means never having to say it's too hot."

"What?"

"Joke."

"Too hot for jokes."

"If we wait for a cool day," I said, "we'll never fuck."

"In California, they have air conditioning?"

"Oh yeah."

"In my next life, I will own two air conditioners and a swimming pool."

"See you in California, baby."

"I will fuck you like crazy in California then."

"Mmmmm."

"We will never get there," she predicted.

"I'll get you to California if it's the last thing I do."

"It's to think of a dream."

"Do you want to help me kill a nun?" I ran my finger up her naked chubby thigh and paused at the edge of her dark wet bush.

"Sure." She blew smoke. "I hate them like shit."

"In New Jersey."

"I don't like it." She leaned over to squash the cigarette in a battered tuna fish can.

"You don't understand. It's a state."

"A steak?"

I rested my forefinger at her dark fleshy opening, and it was wet, she wanted me, she was a liar. I rolled onto one elbow and kissed her chapped lips. "Please?"

"Be fast, get over it, I am sweating."

I put my thing inside her slow and easy.

She grunted. "Why fuck, ouch, in the hot of day?"

"I'm perverse," I said.

"What you say?"

I just lay there on top of her, enjoying it, you can't get any closer than this, naked to our own lies, needy, sweaty, we are such an awful species, hairless gorillas.

Here we were, face to face, body to body, a strange, damaged and unlikely couple. Who could have predicted we would even meet, never mind bare our bodies, souls and pointless dreams? I had never felt so intimate with anyone as with this chubby, angry reject.

We wanted out of here, that was what we had in common.

Was that all we had?

Was it love? Two lost souls coupling?
Or just an electric signal from dick to brain?
"Feels nice inside you," I said.
"For you, perhaps."
"You don't like it ever?"
"Sometimes, I'll say that."
I chanted: "*Sícut érat in princípio, et nunc, et sémper.*"
Finally, she gave a grunt of pleasure.
"*Et in saécula saeculórum,*" she muttered.
"*Amén,*" I said.
Flash.
Not an orgasm.
A brilliant stroke like lightning.
Brightest white.
Silent moment.

A thud, a single terrible bass note, lower than anything ever heard in music. A shock wave rolled through the room like an earth tremor, rattling everything we had.

I leaped up, rushed to the balcony and stood naked at the grenade screen. It had suddenly become flecked with glass and metal shrapnel.

Merci appeared beside me naked but for a T-shirt. Below us, soldiers stumbled, running away from the smoking Marilyn Monroe café.

Merci screamed: "Sanny!"

Down the stairs she raced, half naked, while I scrambled into shorts, dug through the rice jar for her tiny revolver. Weapon off safety, I pounded down the dark stairway, burst through the battered steel door and out into the street.

Mr. Kinh, the gasoline vendor, grabbed Sanny by the wrists and dragged her like a limp doll, over the sidewalk and into the gutter. Sanny, breathing in gasps, was bleeding from the ears.

Now bare-assed Merci leaned over her.

Wounded bleeding Arvin soldiers stumbled around, gasping, shouting in Vietnamese, one of them collapsing with a dull head-cracking thud onto the muddy street. GIs and locals swarmed around us, dazed, choking on nasty cordite fumes. Whatever kind of bomb or grenade had been thrown, it had turned the café's glassware into a thousand pieces of shrapnel, and the muddy street was littered with shards.

The nurse-nun Sister Helena appeared from who knows where and pushed Mr. Kinh aside.

She shouted orders in French. I watched stunned and stupid as she unzipped Sanny's dirty white barmaid dress down to the waist.

No bleeding.

"*Couverture!*" the nun shouted at Merci.

"*Trop chaud,*" Merci answered.

"Blanket, goddamn it," I shouted at Merci, "she's going into shock."

Every combat vet has seen it. If I were writing honest bereavement letters, many would say: *Your son died of shock before the medics could get to him.*

Beside me, an Arvin sergeant lifted a twisted café chair from atop a moaning bloody comrade.

The nun, her white skirt blood-spattered now, turned that chair around and used it to elevate Sanny's bare feet. I slipped Merci's useless revolver into my pocket.

"Ambulance," I shouted. "GI ambulance!"

Merci scrambled into the steam bath and returned with a pile of white towels and she and the nun wrapped Sanny up in them.

Sanny's teeth were chattering behind blue lips, her legs jerking and quivering like she was trying to run.

I waved down a Red Cross ambulance just as it turned the corner. As it honked its way through the crowd, I leaped on the running board.

"Girl's going into shock," I shouted at the driver. "Eardrums. Bleeding."

I led two medics carrying an olive drab stretcher to where Sanny lay, wrapped in towels, Merci on the ground holding her head. Sister Helena had lost her kerchief, revealing GI-style buzz-cut hair, and was hunched over inside the café working on a moaning Arvin soldier.

"Don't hold her head up!" I shouted at Merci.

Then at the medic I yelled: "The girl first."

"You don't tell us, fuck face," said the medic.

He looked at his partner, surveyed the wounded and muttered: "Girl first."

I lapsed into a head-humming state, a dull siren wailing in my brain. The ambulance backed through the crowd, horn honking, the medics shouting and cursing the bystanders, and then they loaded Sanny in, a nurse inside jiggling IV lines.

One wounded bleeding Arvin was loaded, and then another, and then the last one, brought limping to the ambulance by the French Sister, her white blouse smeared in bloody mud.

The medics examined an Arvin boy in the street, with no obvious wounds, maybe sixteen years on this awful planet, abandoned for dead now as the medics hustled toward the ambulance.

They wanted to get the hell out of there before somebody else threw a grenade.

Merci leaped into the ambulance but the Army nurse pushed her out. Away drove the ambulance, bouncing through the potholes, siren whooping.

Merci stood tottering, bare ass turned to me, then collapsed sobbing, prone in the mud, arms out, like she was trying to hold on to the Earth but it was slipping out of her desperate grasp.

I ran upstairs to get her a pair of shorts, and snag my cigarettes and lighter.

Down on the street again, I slipped shorts around Merci as if she were a doll. They were my fatigue shorts, and went on easy. Now dressed in oversize GI clothes, and crying, she looked like a war orphan.

Actually, she *was* a war orphan.

I helped her turn over and held her head in my lap. She had cried herself dry and was blubbering.

I lit a Blend stick and sucked in smoke, slipped the cigarette between her lips and she inhaled.

Gawkers passed us murmuring in three languages. Two curious dogs, frightened away by the blast, perhaps scenting blood now, peered out of the alley and stared at us. Whatever had exploded inside the cafe, it was much more powerful than a frag grenade. The percussion had knocked the sign depicting Marilyn Monroe from its moorings, and it had landed face up in the mud.

Marilyn Monroe, America's most beautiful face, splashed with blood, and still grinning.

"They got Sanny in time," I said to Merci, lying hypocrite that I was. "She'll be in the GI hospital. They'll take good care of her."

But I had no idea what would happen to Sanny.

Merci blew a stream of smoke through quivering lips.

I said: "They'll fatten that skinny girl up, they'll spoil her with steak and mashed potatoes, you'll see."

I was fending off reality with bullshit, stroking my girlfriend's sobbing face, sitting in the glassy smoky debris. Above me a flapping banner advertised a Hollywood movie.

But this wasn't Hollywood.

I was no Ryan O'Neal.

And this was no Love Story.

CHAPTER FIFTEEN

I have this vision of myself, standing outside the Marilyn Monroe with Merci's stainless steel revolver.

I am pointing that revolver at I don't know what, looking for an enemy, a target, anything, as vile smoke envelops bloody chaos.

Any fool can pull a trigger. That was a saying you'd often hear from weary grunts. I could not shake that scene, starring me as the Fool, standing there useless, as that French nun, and our medics, saved the lives of four people.

I met that nun briefly at 7th Surgical Hospital when she stopped by to check on Sanny. I learned that yes, her name was Sister Helena, and although she said nothing about herself, a nurse later told me that Sister Helena was fifty-some years old, a native of Lyon, France, spoke six languages and was suffering from leukemia.

What she was doing on Cong Ly Street at sundown, no one could say, although it was likely she was checking on her prostitute patients.

After visiting Sanny, I stood on the veranda of the Viet Wing of 7th Surgical Infirmary, waiting for the docs to discharge her. They had given her pain medications and promised to release her that afternoon. Her hearing might come back, the doc said, as ruptured ear drums often healed on their own. If not, there were medical tricks they could try.

Sanny, as it turns out, had seen the bomb roll in and had ducked behind the sandbagged counter, saving her own life. All she remembered was a blob bound in black electrical tape, spinning on the floorboards. It seemed to spin for hours, she said, and she tucked up into a ball and everything became very beautiful and very quiet.

She said she wished she could go back to that moment, of beauty and death and peace, since she had awoken to a world of dizziness, throbbing pain and a screech in her head that wouldn't go away.

Alone on the hospital's screened veranda, I lit a stick of the Blend.

Sanny wasn't nearly as messed up as the wounded children lying in beds all around her, some of them amputees, and I could take this rotten war only when I put those children out of my mind.

Smoke puff inhale.

We didn't mean to do it, Your Honor. We were trying to save their country.

Weren't we?

Skinner burst out of the ward, banging the screen door behind me.

"Tough to look at," I said.

"Give me a hit of that shit," Skinner said. "Poor saps."

I passed him the smoldering cigarette. "Lot of pain in there."

"Modern medicine," said Skinner, "ain't it fantastic? Half those kids'd be dead, wasn't for us."

"The children's what you hate to see."

"VC fucking up a whole generation, all's I'm saying." He exhaled smoke. "Blowing up their own kids. How do you like that?"

"What the fuck are we doing here, Skinner, what is the point of all this destruction? Tell me."

"Just say fuck it and drive on. Hey, it sucks man, that's why we gotta win this thing. Listen," Skinner slapped me on the back, "Our cartons?"

"What about 'em?"

"I don't want them delivered in a shit truck.

"Wrapped in plastic, lots and lots of plastic."

"Hey, some of that weed is going to touch my lips."

"Here's the thing...".

"We're under the gun, right? Time-wise? Now think, Peckfogle, what did we just see?"

"A ward full of wounded children."

"No, I mean what happened on Cong Ly Street." He smacked me in the shoulder. "Opportunity! American charity, nothing like it, right? You get wounded, and if you're close to base, and a GI vouches for you, you get good old American health care at 7th Surgical, right?"

"Maybe, if you're lucky and they have a spare bed."

"So we fake an accident, right on Main Gate Road."

"And..."

"We load our fake victim into an ambulance, along with his knapsack, which just happens to contain two cartons of Blend."

I stared at him. Red stubble beard, dark eyes, sweaty face, floppy boonie hat held on by a string.

"Your plan stinks," he said, "mine doesn't, all's I'm saying."

Skinner the heartless.

Skinner the genius.

The Doc appeared on the porch and sniffed the air and knew we were dopers. I saw in his eyes the desire for Blend, but he couldn't lower himself to our level.

He said Sanny felt dizzy, and they intended to keep her another day, and who the hell was she to me anyway?

I said she's my wife's cousin and the Doc gave me a disgusted look, like Sanny was my underage whore. He sneered and retreated into the ward.

We hopped into Skinner's jeep, ripped along the streets of the base, were waved through the gate by Freckles the MP, and drove down Freedom Highway toward Cong Ly Street.

"What's with you and the gook babes, anyway?" Skinner asked as we blew past a convoy of deuce-and-a-halfs.

"You don't need to call them gooks, Skin."

"I mean she's old enough to be your mother."

"Merci? Not quite."

"And she's ugly."

"You see ugly, I see cute."

"And she's fat."

"I'd say plump."

"I don't know, Peckfogle, guy like you, hooking up with foreign women, it looks … weak. I guess. Weak, all's I'm saying."

"It's genetics."

"It's what?"

"Peckfogle genetics. I'm hoping to dilute the fucked-up Peckfogle gene. Inserting an exotic blend of Corsican-Cambodian into the Peckfogle line. It can only help. My kids will have a chance in this world, Skinner. My Mom's Irish, and Merci's Corsican and Cambodian, will outflank the Peckfogle."

"What nationality is Peckfogle, anyway?"

"Nobody knows anymore."

"German, Swedish, what?"

"I'll settle for Hun."

"What's a Hun?"

"Like in Attila. The. Hun."

"How much of that shit you been smoking?"

"You've never heard of Atlilla the Hun?"

"On TV, right?"

"I can imagine the look on my father's face when I bring Merci back to Bayway and announce she's pregnant."

"She's pregnant?"

"I'll get around to that."

"Take my advice, use a rubber."

"I'm a bareback rider all the way."

"So, that's it. That's your play. Make your old man livid by producing a gook grandson. Slap in the face."

"Go easy on the gook stuff. My son is going to be a gook someday."

Skinner snorted and rubbed his red beard. "Not me," he said, "never fucked one, never will. Don't want no tropical diseases. I'll hold out for a round-eye, back in the World."

"Here we go," I said. "Parking spot!"

We parked outside the Marilyn Monroe, and were immediately surrounded by shoeshine boys and begging girls with their little palms turned up.

"Which one of these little fuckers has the grenade?" muttered Skinner. He untangled himself from the jeep, removed his boonie hat and used it to swat away the children.

I fixated on the steering wheel and gas pedal. I could put Merci in this jeep and we could drive to ... things were dicey in Cambodia. How far was Bangkok?

A boy tugged on my arm.

He wore an enormous floppy hat that shaded his face. He was a year or two short of puberty, but already a pimp.

"Short time, GI?" He held up five dirty fingers. "Five dollar, my sister, very pretty."

The other street urchins watched in envy.

"Fuck you," I said.

The boy spit on my shirt. I leaped out of the jeep and ran after him as the street urchins screeched in joy and fear. I let the kid disappear down Madame Ba Gi's alley, and turned back for the Marilyn Monroe.

Aside from a few singe marks, you'd never know the cafe had just been bombed. Next door, the banner that said STEAM BATH MASSAGE had been torn loose and was flapping in the sweltering breeze. Skinner slouched in the scant shade of the massage parlor's doorway.

"You ought to give 'er a name. Something sexy," Skinner said.

"What?"

"Your business."

"It's not mine."

"It's your sweetheart's, right? Take it over. Be a man. You're pussy whipped, Peckfogle."

"The business doesn't belong to her, she manages it, that's all."

"How about, Hand Job Paradise."

"Undignified. Not gonna fly with Merci."

"I got the slogan: We jerk, you squirt."

My rejoinder was cut short as Du Ky walked out of the Marilyn Monroe. He was framed in sunlight like a ragged dirty saint.

In America, the terrorist bombing of a café would bring a month of breathless news coverage and demands for a Congressional investigation. Meanwhile the site would be turned into a memorial, its eternal flame illuminating a stack of wrongful-death lawsuits.

But this wasn't America. After the grenade attack on the Marilyn Monroe, Mister Tin and his Arvin son swept up the debris, wiped away the blood stains, restocked the beer cooler, bought new cups, plates, bowls and glasses, and reopened the next afternoon. They replaced the shrapnel-shattered menu boards, and took that opportunity to raise prices.

Du Ky hopped into the back seat of the jeep, Skinner eased behind the wheel and I called shotgun.

"Du Ky, Skinner. Skinner, Du Ky."

Skinner ignored Du Ky's outstretched hand, recoiling like Du Ky had leprosy.

"He's our ace translator," I said.

"Fuck a bunch of coconut-sucking monkeys," said Skinner. "How do you say that in Vietnamese?"

Du Ky, how ever much of that insult he understood, only smiled.

"Who's he gonna translate for?" Skinner asked.

"The honey wagon driver."

"No shit truck, I told you already."

"Skinner."

"Absolutely not, last and final word, all's I'm saying."

Women in ao dais, men in uniform, children in rags squeezed between our jeep and the door of the massage parlor. Any one of them could have dropped a grenade. If I was grenade-paranoid before, I was frantic now, watching hands as the locals walked by.

"Okay, Skinner, the clock's ticking, what's your plan then?"

Du Ky, in the back seat, shifted his floppy hat to keep the wicked sun out of his eyes. "They shoot horses, don't they?" he said.

"What the fuck's he talking about?" asked Skinner.

"I would like to see it," said Du Ky.

"He's a movie buff," I said.

"They made a movie about shooting horses?" Skinner asked.

"Jane Fonda," said Du Ky. "Big star."

"She rides a horse?" asked Skinner.

"She plays a loser of dancing," said Du Ky.

"Look," said Skinner. "I don't go to movies, let's talk about the plan. Now you go up and down the market, and there's people slaughtering chickens and ducks, right?"

"Right," I said.

"We splash chicken blood over your friend here, and we call the medics. Maybe we claim we saw VC, and we fire off a couple of rounds to make it authentic. We stage this close to the Main Gate, so there's no question. This gravely wounded man …"

Skinner hiked his thumb back toward Du Ky.

"… a friend to many GIs, will be treated at the United States Army 7th Surgical. When we load this poor blood-splashed sap into ambulance, we throw in his backpack. The ambulance boys drive that backpack through the gate. Bingo!"

"All right," I said. "Maybe."

"I'm a fucking genius," said Skinner, "if I do say so myself."

"How about it Du Ky?" I asked. "Are you willing to be splashed with chicken blood?"

"How much?"

"Oh a pint would do it," said Skinner.

"No, how much dollars?" asked Du Ky.

"Ten," said Skinner. "I'm feeling generous."

"Twenty," I said. "Come on."

"That's a week's pay over here," Skinner objected.

"Twenty five," said Du Ky.

"That's fair," I insisted.

"Comes out of your pocket, big spender," Skinner grumbled.

"Skinner, we've got a deadline here, may I remind you. A Binh Xuyen gangster is threatening to cut off Merci's fingers."

"A pinky, is that a big deal?"

"It's a big deal if it's your girlfriend."

"Nah. Crocodile needs us. What do you think, Mister Translator?"

Du Ky looked around in caution and whispered, "Crocodile is a danger man."

"No," Skinner said, "what do you think of our ambulance plan?"

"I am not so sure," said Du Ky. "What happens when I get inside the hospital?"

"You make like Lazarus, and sneak away," Skinner said. "Nobody in there's going to give a shit about a ... a cyclo driver."

"They're pretty busy in there," I admitted. "It's the chaos clinic. They'll probably just shrug it off."

"Write a report, if that," said Skinner.

"Tell you what," I said. "Let's go around the corner and get our fortunes told."

"You believe in that crap?" Skinner asked.

"Let's see if she's open first," I said.

But that was a sneaky lie. I had other motivations.

Ba Gi the tarot card reader worked out of a tent in an alley just across from the neighborhood's most expensive whorehouse. Crocodile called it the *Café de Prostitutes*, but its official name was the Perfume Club. Only Vietnamese criminals or American construction workers could afford to whore there, and I'd never been up those pricey stairs.

Ba Gi's tent was pure white and made of American parachutes sewn together. She had a spooky reputation on Cong Ly Street because she always seemed to close her business just before bad things happened.

But now her tent was open.

I slipped in, calling: "Ba?"

A man of my age did not call a much older Vietnamese woman by first name. It was *Ba*, grandmother, a term of ultimate respect. She was a beautiful old lady with her head wrapped in a white rag. She had the smooth skin of a girl, and big eyes that shone with something, maybe kindness, maybe understanding, maybe greed.

The old-time Viets didn't need chairs and Ba Gi squatted behind her display table, which was actually a soldier's footlocker.

On that table, tarot cards had been placed in four stacks alongside an ashtray scattered with remnants of incense sticks.

It smelled heavenly in her tent.

I sat on a milk carton across from her.

She wore a shiny green blouse and black pajama trousers. Her lips barely moved when she said: "GI lucky day, fifty cents."

I patted my chest. "Not for me, grandmother."

She levitated her hands over the cards.

"For my friend Du Ky," I said, "the cyclo driver, you know him. He feels bad and needs a cheerful reading."

Ba Gi gave the slightest nod.

I said: "Good fortune, you *bic*?"

Her hands settled on the cards.

"Nice words," I said. "Nice. How do you say it? *Tot?*"

"*Da.*"

"I'll give you two dollars, then I bring him here for a good fortune." I produced the greenbacks. "Good luck for Du Ky."

"Okay," she said, and flipped over a top card.

Ace of Swords.

Whatever that meant.

She looked through me with those deep dark eyes.

"Bring," she said.

While Skinner lounged at a café table under the shrapnel-torn awning of the Marilyn Monroe drinking warm beer, I escorted Du Ky to the tarot reader's tent. I felt pretty sure Ba Gi would keep my bribe a secret. As Du Ky walked in for a private reading, I climbed the balcony stairs of the Perfume Club and there, surrounded by three half-naked teenage prostitutes, sat Crocodile.

He was the only man in the place.

He hissed at the prostitutes and they scattered.

He occupied a table that had a lacquered top depicting a golden dragon. Atop that table was a pack of Kools and a glowing red cabaret candle.

I pulled out a chair and he fixed me with his good eye.

"My prince," he said.

"What?"

"Prince of GIs."

I sat down. A breeze, deflected off the surrounding rooftops, slithered in and cooled my sweaty forehead.

"Speck Focal, you look heated."

"I was at the GI hospital this morning."

"So?"

"The girl, the waitress, she's dizzy and in very bad pain."

"Tell me, Speck Focal, you Catholics believe in God. Why did he create pain?"

I spread my hands in a helpless gesture.

"Why did he create leprosy, and all its suffering?" he asked.

My lips moved, but produced no worthwhile sound.

"God is evil," Crocodile said, "that is the big answer."

"I'm no philosopher."

"Oh no? I believe you were a … what is the word, aspiring … that is what to say, correct? Aspiring poet."

"Who told you that?"

"Aspire, I believe to be from the French word."

"Oh, Merci must have told you that."

Suddenly paranoid, I thought: What conversations have Crocodile and Merci had about me?

"No philosophy, no poetry," he said. "Wouldn't you say?"

"You missed your calling, Crocodile, you should have been a professor."

"A boy who is rejected as diseased, he has much private time, for study and thought. No branch of human inquiry has escaped me, and I have found that all of it is … futile."

"We're smuggling our cartons through the gate today. Tomorrow, we have seed money."

"Futile, from the French, by the way. Words that are both English and French intrigue me. So many worthwhile things are French in origin, wouldn't you agree?" He put his finger stumps to his mouth and kissed them in a flash of golden teeth.

"Perhaps," he said, "we will all get rich and your whore will keep her fingers."

I felt like I had grabbed a live electric wire. I said: "You don't need to threaten her."

"It is not threatening, Speck Focal. Crocodile is a just and fair man, ask anyone on the street. Ask any whore if I have ever harmed her without cause. Those who play by the rules ..." he waved his leprosy-wounded fingers, "have no fear of Crocodile."

That's not what I'd heard. He was infamous for mutilating the hands of prostitutes who displeased him.

He twirled that pack of Kools. "Fair and square, as your John Wayne says."

I fished a half smoked Blend out of my fatigue shirt pocket, lit it from the candle, walked two paces to the edge of the balcony and blew smoke into the breeze. The white tent, flap closed now, contained Ba Gi and Du Ky and Fate.

With a puff of the Blend and my anxiety faded, replaced by a vision of the big ceramic rice jar in Merci's apartment. Merci kept two months rice rations, in fear of starvation. Also in there was her .32 revolver, a pea-shooter really, but at close range a good-enough assassin's weapon. Although I was a typewriter warrior now, I had endured nearly six months of frightening night ambushes and exhausting day sweeps, and despite all my internal feelings of cowardice, I had not run under fire. I had dropped into prone, just as I had been trained to. I had fired at the enemy, if only in blind fear, but I had done it. I, cowardly warrior, survivor of VC ambushes, could assassinate Crocodile if I had to.

Crocodile was either a fatalist or a fool, for he had many enemies but was rarely accompanied by one of his thugs. It was a macho thing. He wanted to show he needed no protection. He considered me harmless, which gave me a sneaky advantage.

I choked on my own smoke.

"Speck Focal," Crocodile said, "I have ordered you a beer."

I waved that off, kept my back turned to him.

Consequences?

I'd be interrogated by MPs. I had been through the process. My fellow prisoners at LBJ had taught me how to cope. You simply answer their questions with questions. Unless you're a special case, your interrogators are just looking to fill in the blanks of their reports. You give them something, anything to write down, and they grow bored with the game soon enough. So yes, I could cope with the interrogation. Merci's pistol, cheap and illegal, was not traceable to me or her. I would leave no witnesses, for after ten at night Cong Ly street belongs only to criminals and blind-drunk GIs.

However, unless I completed the drug deal, I'd have nothing to trade Colonel Sadler in return for my freedom. He would lose any obligation to me and I'd be staying in Vietnam for quite a while. My mom would be locked in an Idaho prison. Merci would have to go into hiding far away, maybe all the way to Phnom Penh, in fear that Crocodile's thugs would slit her throat.

And she hated Phnom Penh, the city where her mother and father met.

I needed this drug deal to come off. I needed to expose Crocodile's "inside man" on our base. I needed to give Merci bribe money so she could buy a visa and fly to California. I needed cash to bail out the crazy holy peacenik I called Mom.

And I needed to get the fuck out of this war.

The Inner Raging Peckfogle, the millionth descendent of Atilla the Hun, wanted to blow Crocodile's brains out. But Peckfogle the Catholic schoolboy and reluctant warrior?

"Can't do it," I muttered.

Crocodile, stepping up behind me, put something shocking cold against the back of my neck. For a moment I thought it was a pistol but it turned out to be a bottle of beer.

He said: "Ice-chilled, just as you Americans like it."

I spun around, looked him in the eye.

"Miller High Life." He handed me the bottle. "Only the best for you, Speck Focal."

"Just can't do it," my lips said.

I set that bottle on the table, my hands shaky.

"Too early for drink?" Crocodile asked. "Indigestion again? You ought to see a doctor for your problem."

CHAPTER SIXTEEN

My parole guy, Warrant Officer Tom Brennan, is a lifer, but not an asshole.

He's a tall, pale, blue-eyed Scandnavian type, the Colonel's man all the way, a weightlifter, a rabid fan of the Green Bay Packers, and an officer with the Criminal Investigation Division, which is sort of the Army's FBI.

Last month, when he escorted me from LBJ to Captain Clark's office for reassignment as a typist, he indulged me with a stop at the PX.

For a Three Musketeers Bar.

Actually, I ate three of them right there.

Which means I ate 9 Musketeers.

The PX is air conditioned, the only place for miles around where you can get unmelted candy. You have no idea how much you crave crappy American candy until you've spent a month in LBJ.

Now Brennan was my secret conduit to Colonel Sadler, and I trusted this guy, he was straight up and strack.

Our rendezvous was the ammo dump.

There was a reason we met there. The ammo dump was off by itself on the sandy perimeter road, just beyond the morgue. It was surrounded by hills of sandbags, and beside an artificial lake meant to aid in the hopeless task of fighting a fire should the ammo start cooking off.

You wouldn't want to be a firefighter on that day.

Given the VC talent for slinging mortar rounds, nobody wanted to be anywhere near the ammo dump at any time, day or night. Everything within 1000 yards would be either blown to pieces or cut up by BBs, shrapnel, and flechette arrows. Just one white phosphorous mortar round would turn the ammo dump into a tiny nuclear bomb.

So there was nobody else around when I met Brennan in the shadow of the ammo dump's abandoned guard shack. It was just sundown, hottest part of the day. He drove up in a shiny jeep with no insignia, no numbers, nothing, just olive paint and a radio antenna.

"What do you have for me?" Brennan asked. His face was an overheated shade of red, although his uniform was laundry-starched and his hair perfectly clipped around a billed cap.

The wicked sun threw long shadows and the breeze smelled of pond scum, hot steel and road dust. The jeep engine rattled like the end of a greasy, four-cylinder symphony.

I swung into the seat beside Brennan, so we could talk without eyeball contact.

"Need your help," I said.

"Fire away."

"Tomorrow I need to get two cartons through. Trial run."

"Okay."

"Four in the afternoon, there'll be a rickshaw 'accident' on Freedom Road. One cyclo driver hits the dust, maybe a GI passenger too. Ambo will be called. The driver's backpack, that's what we need to get in."

"Got it."

"The fake victim's going to walk out of the clinic. The medics will report that. The report needs to be ditched."

Brennan held the steering wheel with both hands, like he was eager to drive off. "What about the main deal?" he asked.

"So wait, the MPs, they're going to let this ambo through, right?"

"Don't worry about the MPs. What about the main deal?"

"It comes down a few days after those first two cartons get in. Profit from the two cartons finances the main deal."

"Names?"

"We'll see what buyers appear. Apparently there's one mystery man on this base who distributes Crocodile's drugs."

"And who would that be?"

I shrugged. "Whoever it is, they've got a mountain of cash. We're talking fifty grand in greenbacks, paid from the mystery man direct to Crocodile. I don't get to touch the big money."

Brennan stared at the sundown horizon. It was glowing red-orange, suggesting smooth sailing tomorrow.

I said: "So this suggests to me ..."

"Do tell, Private Peckfogle."

"... somebody at the Casino. Who else has that kind of cash?"

"Outstanding," said Brennan. "Anything else? Because we don't want to be seen here, do we?"

"What about my casino theory?"

"We watch that casino like a hawk watches a chicken coop."

I saluted him, flashing the FTA.

Brennan shook his head.

"Peckfogle," he said. "you're a born civilian."

When I straggled back to my sandbagged Dead Letter Bunker, Skinner awaited in the dark, illuminated only by gas lantern.

"Where you been?"

"PX," I lied.

"You didn't buy nothing?"

"Just looking," I said. "Short of cash."

"PX closes at 5, right? Like an hour-some ago."

"What's this, the Inquisition? I once had a nun like you."

"Here, fucker, explain this."

He handed me a torn envelope, one of mine, addressed to Miss Constance Malecki, 625 Pulaski Street, Apartment B, Bayway N.J.

I pulled out the letter. I read it dumbfounded. I read the whole thing, unwilling to believe it actually was my letter and that Skinner had intercepted it at the Post Office.

Dear Miss Malecki:

I can't say as I blame you for ignoring my last letter.
You probably remember me as a jerky schoolboy.
Wipe that image out of your mind.
You're not married are you?
The thought just occurred to me.

Anyway, I assure you I am not the snot-nose kid you remember.

I am now engaged in a secret undercover operation on behalf of the United States Army in Vietnam. I cannot say more about my mission, only that it is both dangerous and critical to the Army's purpose here.

I am writing to you because there's a distinct possibility that my service will come to a rather abrupt end. The details are classified, but these patriotic combat boots could be walking American soil as soon as next week.

Although I have no intention of resettling in Bayway, Miss Malecki, I have thought of you quite often during my service to our nation. You were the only kind-hearted teacher at Saint Sebastian's.

I think I love you, as stated in previous missives. Would it be possible for us to meet upon my return to civilian life?
Very truly yours
Captain John Jay Peckfogle, United States Army.

"Secret undercover operation?" Skinner said.

I folded the letter.

"So now what?" Skinner said. "You're a fucking captain? What's going on here?"

"Skinner, man..."

"Don't Skinner man me. What the fuck, Peckfogle?"

"It's embarrassing, okay?"

"Oh it's more than fucking embarrassing. What's undercover? What does that mean?"

He pulled his service forty-five out of its holster and held it upside my nose. I could see far down the barrel. It smelled like rat shit, dynamite and the Bayway refinery.

"Are you narking on me, motherfucker?"

I stuttered: "I'm trying to impress a blonde back home with bullshit. You know me, Skinner, I'm a bullshit artist."

With my index finger, I gently pushed the gun barrel away from my face. "Come on, man, am I supposed to tell this Jersey girl I'm a drug dealer? If I pretend to be James Bond, I have a better chance of getting laid once I get back to Bayway."

"Where you're gonna be next week? What about your gook broad? All of a sudden you're going home?"

"FTA's my ticket out of here," I said, and saluted. "They're going to slap me with a dishonorable and put me on the street. That's the word."

Skinner holstered his weapon. "Word from who?"

"The MPs at the gate told me."

"You are full of shit. I ought to plug you right now, right here, it ain't but ten steps to a pile of coffins."

"Can't blame a guy for trying to game a blonde, can you Skinner?"

He flicked the light switch and this time the overhead worked, flooding the room with harsh rays.

"Who's the blonde?"

"Used to be my high school teacher."

"You sick vegetarian fuck. You're horny for a nun?"

"No!"

"She taught Catholic school but she wasn't a nun?"

"Only half of ... "

Skinner stomped out. There really is no ordinary doorway to my hovel but a zig-zag passage built of sandbags. I heard his jeep grind to a start and begin to clatter.

I held the Miss Malecki letter in a sweaty hand.

I knew then that I didn't have the nerve for intelligence work.

I could still smell the steely oil of Skinner's pistol, and I needed to take a wicked piss.

As I turned to douse the lantern's flame, I heard an ominous sound on the floorboards, a rolling and wobbling like an out of shape bowling ball. I knew what it was even before I saw the handgrenade skitter across the floor and wobble to a stop just at the foot of my bunk.

I stared at it.

Goodbye, Mom. I hope ...

And then everything went dark.

I awoke on the floor next to my bunk, the handgrenade inches from my nose. I have never seen anything so clearly as when my eyes focused on the cotter pin, still in its place in the handle.

A wave of extreme heat passed through me.

Skinner kicked me in the ribs.

I rolled over and was looking at his boots, his fatigue trousers bloused into their shiny tops.

"I catch you in one lie, and you are dead," he growled. "I pull the pin next time, all's I'm saying."

CHAPTER SEVENTEEN

I told myself Skinner needed me, and would not blow me up, at least not before the Main Deal. He and Crocodile hated each other, and I was the only intermediary who could make this work.

I told myself this, but spent the entire next morning transforming my bunk into a bomb shelter. I pushed the bunk away from the wall, to give me a space to drop into, and I sandbagged it on three sides.

Still, my quarters had no door and I gave myself only a fifty-fifty chance the next time a grenade rolled in here. Even if I managed to scramble underneath my bed-bunker, men had bled to death from the blast of a grenade in tight quarters.

Bled from the ears, and died of shock, as would have happened to Sanny except for the Miracle of Sister Helena.

In the event of my fragging, I wondered, who would write the phony bereavement letter to my mom? Would he type it on my Underwood?

Anxiety plus sandbagging equals sweat, and once I competed my sandbagging labors I needed a shower and of course the water tank at Graves Registration had run dry. I walked a hot half mile along the dusty streets of ~~Sacramento~~ Long Binh and headed for the pool, which had the best showers on the base, actual running water.

Ordinarily I avoided the pool, which was refreshing only if you liked standing chest-to-chest with enlisted men in hot bleached water, not one goddamned female in sight.

Ninety percent of the reason to go swimming is girls in bathing suits.

This part of Long Binh reminded me strongly of Sacramento, where I, strangely enough, have a history. My big brother Ben Franklin lived in a commune at the west edge of that bland urban sprawl. The first stage of my trip to Vietnam was a United flight from Philly to Oakland, and rather than report directly to the Army Terminal, I looked up Ben.

As big brother, he'd taken the worst of our father's whippings, and upon reaching the age 18 he hugged Mom, announced he was leaving the family forever, and that none of us would hear from him again.

So I went AWOL in Oakland to find him.

It wasn't hard.

Mom had his address.

I stayed with Ben for 29 days, because after 30 days, an AWOL soldier becomes a deserter.

Ben and I smoked a lot of dope, cursed our father in every way imaginable, made day trips to Haight-Ashbury, sat dope-addled in Golden Gate Park, ate at Indian vegetarian restaurants, discovered the delights of Hippie Girl Love, and on our last day together, hitch-hiked across the Golden Gate Bridge and climbed Mount Tamalpais. At the peak of said mountain I decided to become an impoverished San Francisco poet.

Should I survive the coming Asian debacle.

Ben and I departed friends, but he asked me not to look for him ever again.

"I have renounced Adam Peckfogle," he said, "and all his works and pomps."

"I'm one of his pomps?" I said.

"Goodbye, Jay," my brother said. "This time it's forever."

I later heard from Mom that, despite our 29 days of friendship, Ben was very upset that I had found him. Spooked, he had moved to Baja and taken up surfing.

The bully Adam Peckfogle had destroyed his family and had driven them, literally in Ben's case, to the ends of the Earth.

I felt a sad weight mulling that history, but it was somewhat relieved by a few minutes in the pool's glorious shower, under actual piped-in water with cool concrete under my feet. The pool's EM club served excellent French Fries, which I sprinkled with malt vinegar and consumed poolside.

The EM pool was noisy, crowded and its water had an oily sheen. But across a green chain link fence was its upscale twin, the officer's pool. In its cool clean water splashed only eight or ten men in swim trunks. Over there, on loungers, lay three actual females, in modest swimsuits, nurses I supposed.

The men were playing water polo, and on the near side of the net I recognized W2 Brennan and his mentor, Colonel Sadler.

I slurped the last of my ice tea and walked to that fence and grasped it. For the first time I acknowledged an unseemly truth. I wanted to be on the other side. Not here with the rubes and rednecks, but over there, with the officers.

With the cool guys.

With the Collegiates.

Who made the big money.

Who had all the good things.

Over here warm Carling Black Label.

Over there, cold Budweiser.

Over here, ceiling fans.

Over there, air conditioning.

They gave the orders, we did the grunt work. They slept in hootches, while infantry guys wrapped themselves in ponchos in the boonies. When the nurses hung out, it was always with the ranking guys.

I focused on the letters FTA inked on my fence-grasping hand. I could get them inked over but that would not erase my hatred for authority, beaten into me by a jockey's crop.

I roused myself from the worthless swamp of self pity and hitch-hiked over to 7th Surgical to visit Sanny.

But she was gone. In her bed was a delirious, writhing Vietnamese boy in bloody sheets, whose leg had been amputated above the knee.

I walked to Main Gate and jived my way through the MP shack, getting the wink-and-nod from Connors, known to all as Freckles the MP. I flipped him a thumbs up which meant I'd pay him off with a Blend stick later, and fended off desperate rickshaw drivers as I sauntered down Freedom Road.

Taking shady shelter under the moldy concrete of what we called First Bridge, I awaited Skinner and pondered the mystery of Sanny.

Her Army nurse, a chubby, cheerful Earth Mother from Virginia, had informed me that Sanny had suffered an inner ear disturbance that made her profoundly dizzy. She was bed-bound and unable to keep a meal down. The doctors here could not treat her, so they had medi-vaced her to Japan.

Japan?

That's what the Army did for wounded GIs, evacuated them to a hospital at Kyoto Air Base.

Sanny was a Vietnamese national.

Wasn't she?

Skinner pulled up while I was mulling this and as I slid into the jeep I said, "Guess what, Skin, the teenage girl who got fragged? Japan."

Skinner shrugged.

"They flew her to Kyoto," I said.

"What do you want from me?"

"Since when do Viet civilians ..."

"Only a jackass tries to make sense out of this man's Army. Just say fuck it and drive on."

He rammed the jeep into gear.

I cannot forget what he looked like that day, with his scant red beard dripping sweat, his ragged sun-bleached boonie hat held tight to his head by its strap. He looked ordinary, that was the striking thing, just another lean young white soldier from middle America, Spec-Four patch on his shoulder, starched uniform, boots shined to a gleam by his hooch maid. At that moment there were at least a hundred thousand guys like him in-country. Except for the fact that he was allowed to grow a stubble of beard, there was nothing special about him, at all.

Along Freedom Road stood a moldy apartment building that was rented to American construction workers, spies, minor diplomats and foreign journalists. We were supposed to rendezvous with Du Ky across from it, but he was a no-show. The plan was Skinner would get into his rickshaw as a passenger, I would *didi-mau* in the jeep, they would overturn the rickshaw, and Du Ky would splash himself with chicken blood.

Everyone in those apartments had a phone, and surely somebody would call the "accident" in.

But we drove up and down Freedom Road for maybe twenty minutes, Skinner cursing me and Du Ky.

Finally in our fourth whirl around the traffic circle, there was Du Ky's rusty rickshaw and we rode behind it. Du Ky puttered away, and we followed, passing the Main Gate, and the apartment building where we were supposed to stage the accident.

"Fuck's he doing?" Skinner called into the slipstream.

"I don't know," I shouted.

Skinner pulled up in the oncoming lane and paced Du Ky. He looked over at us and smiled. He was wearing his pith helmet again, his spirits revived after a cheery Tarot reading.

I'm not sure he realized we had missed the rendezvous point.

We were going maybe forty miles an hour, side by side down an asphalt two-lane road, and when we rounded a river bend, we were the only traffic in sight.

Du Ky thought this was a game and gave his rickshaw full gas.

Skinner too stepped on the gas to keep pace.

And then he swerved and bumped Du Ky off the road.

I turned in the seat to see his rickshaw rolling over on itself, down off the road and into a swamp.

As it flipped and flopped Du Ky held on for maybe three rotations before he came away from it, cycle and carriage parting and rolling over and over, and Du Ky flopping like a rag doll before one final splash into the swamp.

It seemed to take twenty minutes for the rolling and tumbling to stop.

Skinner braked the jeep, looked back, laughed.

"There's your accident. All's I'm saying."

He performed a rapid K-turn in a village alley, and drove back toward the scene of the crime.

I hadn't found a word to say yet.

My eyes had witnessed but my mind would not believe.

Skinner pulled off the road at the scene. The cyclo and carriage were stuck at odd angles in a shallow swamp, but Du Ky himself could not be seen.

Skinner picked up the jeep's radio mic and called Alpha Medic.

I forced myself to get out of the jeep and zombie walk into the swamp. Skinner, just behind me when he reached the rickshaw carriage, held up Du Ky's backpack like it was a trophy fish.

"Got it," he said.

I, zombie, walked on.

Skinner caught up to me, grabbed me by the arm and handed me Du Ky's pack.

"Put it on him," he said. "Get it through. Don't need no rolling ambulance. Fly boys'll be here in a minute."

I walked on, grasping the pack with its two cartons of Blend.

I strung it around my neck.

The swamp was getting deeper.

Muckier.

Pulled at my combat boots.

Every step a slog.

I picked up Du Ky's pith helmet, floating like a boat on the black water.

I plodded on. The muck was so deep and heavy it pulled even the tightly-laced combat boots off my foot. First one, then a few steps later, the other. I was thigh-deep in swamp water, barefoot and nearly knee-deep in muck.

My heavy breathing became gasping in the brutal sun, stinky water, clinging muck.

Du Ky was face down, his neck at a broken angle.

There was only a little blood in the water.

I dropped the pith helmet, grasped his muddy hair and pulled his head up. Water issued from his mouth and nose. His eyes were open but all their humanity was gone.

There was no solid ground to lay him on.

I held him in my arms, he was maybe a buoyant hundred pounds, water draining from the pockets of his second-hand GI uniform.

I was so deep in the muck I could not turn around.

I heard the blades of a med-evac helicopter chopping the air above me.

Somebody was shouting.

Probably me.

My choking screams lost in the overwhelming noise.

And the prop wash was the whirlwind.

CHAPTER EIGHTEEN

With Sanny in the hospital, Quang, Mr. Tin's son, ran the Marilyn Monroe. I made a deal with Quang, using my ration card at the PX to buy two bottles of Jim Beam bourbon, one for me to drink, and one for him to sell, one profitable shot at a time, over the counter.

I drank my bottle, alone, over the next two nights, bunking in Sanny's tight quarters at the back of the café. As part of the deal, Quang ignored me and would not tell anyone, not even Merci, that I was hiding back there. I drank myself to sleep for those two nights and during the day I re-read *On The Road* and played the Tarot, laying out the cards, and studying the pamphlet that came with the pack.

On the second morning, over a breakfast of rice porridge and Sanka, I drew the Hanged Man Card first thing.

Sobering into pain, I stared at the Hanged Man and muttered: *I will get you, Skinner, if it's the last thing I do.*

I could not face Merci, not yet.

I saw it all a hundred times, as hard as I tried to quash the memory. The helicopter with the big red cross on its doors did not airlift Du Ky, since he was dead, and it never did land, but hovered over the body, its prop wash making waves in swamp water. The medics could tell from ten feet up that nothing would save Du Ky and so, wary of landing in the muck, they had flown away, becoming, like Du Ky's soul, a mere speck in the sky.

I shuddered with that memory. I stumbled into the café's pit toilet and puked bile, Tums and Jim Beam.

On the third day I rallied and carried Du Ky's backpack to the traffic circle and waited for Mister Phan and his stinky truck. I felt like the Hanged Man, sunk in the swamp of fatalism. I jettisoned the original, cautious plan of wrapping the cartons in many plastic bags, and dropping them directly into the shit tank. I paid Mister Phan a $20 bribe to take that backpack through the gate, and he flung it casually behind the seat and drove through without even a token inspection from the MPs.

Mr. Phan didn't give a damn because the MPs could only turn him over to the local police, who were puppets of the Binh Xuyen drug gang.

On our end, I attributed this no-hassle smuggling to the influence of W2 Brennan, at work behind the scenes.

I reconnoitered with Mister Phan at his first stop on base, the motor pool latrine, where I retrieved the backpack, walked it to my dark bunker, lit the lantern, and unpacked the cartons.

There next to my Underwood, looking like cartons of factory-produced cigarettes, was dope worth $2000 even at wholesale prices.

The cartons, white with gold trim, depicted a French woman, lying on a couch smoking up a dream, beside her, the words *Le Rêve* in fancy script.

Crocodile was a true professional, you almost had to admire that. No bad doses here, no formaldehyde, no ditch weed, the smoker knew exactly what he was going to get from Crocodile's Blend.

Relief from vile reality.

Who wouldn't pay a few bucks for that?

I for instance was trapped in the reality that I still needed Skinner's cash, that Crocodile had sadistic designs on my girlfriend, that my mom was locked up with perverts in a Pocatello jail.

There really wasn't a lot of time. The packs had to be sold and quickly.

My first stop was the Newbie barracks, presided over by the fat degenerate redneck Staff Sergeant Foster.

He had so far failed in his twin life goals, which were drinking himself to death and gambling himself broke at the casino.

Every thirty days, the Army paid him, and every few weeks, the cargo ships unloaded another pallet of Southern Comfort. Foster, despite all his efforts, could achieve neither bankruptcy nor liver failure.

I found him drunk at his Pepsi cooler.

"Private," he said. "Reach in there and fetch a Pepsi. On me."

His cooler was filled with an assortment of canned soda, but to Foster, every brand was Pepsi, no matter the flavor.

I dipped my hand in almost cold water, hauled up a lukewarm Doctor Pepper, and offered Foster $1 in MPC.

"Keep the change," I said.

"No charge for you, perckerwood," he slurred. He was from Georgia, or maybe Alabama, somewhere with a heavy drawl.

He was alone, as he was twice a day, when the Newbies attended cattle call over in The Pen. There they awaited their fateful assignments, as blasted through loudspeakers.

Pepsis weren't all Foster sold. He'd been a distributor of The Blend for quite a while, selling nervous Newbies a stick of relaxation for up to $25, since they didn't know its fair market value.

I stepped into the shade and drank vile warm soda, which hydration I desperately needed, given my two-day hangover.

"Sarge," I said, "how many sticks could you move?"

"Sticks?"

"Yeah, in packs. Theoretically."

"Hmm," said Foster. "What are we talking?"

He farted grandly into his orange beach chair, lifting one ass cheek and groaning.

"Let's see it," he said.

"I haven't got it on me."

"I mean the tattoo."

Word was getting around the base, but whether this would prove to be my salvation or ruination, I didn't know. I jammed my saluting hand in my pocket. "Don't write me up," I said.

Foster sputtered, coughed and drank from a can of Pepsi that gave off a whiff of sour booze.

"Write you up? What kind of peckerwood do you think I am?"

"I could slip you a pack," I said, "maybe two."

"How much?"

"Factory sealed," I said.

"How much?"

"A hundred per pack, greenbacks, though."

"I'll take it."

"Can you take two?"

"What game you playing, boy?"

"Could you possibly take a carton?"

Silence. It may have been a while since Foster's brain actually indulged in the reasoning process.

"Tell you what," he said. "I can get my hands on $900, no more."

"Nine packs then."

"Boy, ain't you heard of the wholesale discount?"

So we shook hands on a deal for a carton, at a discount, even though I knew Foster could borrow beaucoup cash from his buddies, poker addicts who hung around the casino cheating each other.

As I walked away, the Loudspeakers of Fate were croaking out the final orders of the day.

"Zack. Peter. One-four-seven-two-niner-three. Da Nang, Eleven Bravo."

Da Nang? Infantry?

About a ten percent chance that sometime this year, some lowly clerk at Da Nang would write a bereavement letter beginning: Dear Mr. and Mrs. Zack ...

I got full price for the other packs, as the armorer bought two, the librarian one, the mess sergeant one, and I sold three to my former infantry brethren, one to the PX manager, one in the Commo Shack and one at the Motor Pool. I didn't even try at the casino, figuring SSG Foster had that angle covered. As sundown neared, I stuffed $1900 in good US cash into the sandbag at the base of my blast wall.

Night follows sundown almost immediately in the tropics, and it was full dark by the time I reached the base of Tower 23. Everything was in shadow except for the spot-lit no man's land of concertina wire and land mines. I stood in the deepest shadow below the wooden tower. Skinner was up there, boots scraping the floorboards.

I don't think he knew I was underneath him.

I imagined myself sneaking out there to the twilight edge of the wire, and turning around a Claymore, aiming it at Du Ky's murderer.

In fantasy life, I climbed the ladder, pretended to see VC in the swamp, at which point Skinner would go to the machine gun and I would duck behind the blast wall and clack, Skinner would be dead.

Front toward enemy!

You could get away with murder over here.

Tragic accident of war, VC had turned around the Claymores, happened every day, there'd be only a brief inquiry.

Q: What were you doing out at Tower 23, Peckfogle?
A: Keeping my friend Skinner company, sir, we often played cards out there all night.

It was quite the bubble of fantasy, punctured by my need for Skinner's cash.

"Skinner," I whispered.

Scraping of combat boots.

Skinner leaned over the blast wall. "Scare the fuck out of me, sneaking around. Get up here."

"Just came to say, got two grand, need your end now."

He flipped open the trap door and climbed down the stairs. We walked away from the concertina wire, over the sandy road, into the deepest shadows.

"Cartons sold?" he asked.

"All sold."

"Thanks for coming through, man." He slapped me friendly on the shoulder. "You're a good guy, hey I'm sorry, all's I'm saying."

"I need the rest of the cash."

"And you'll get it. Soon as I get off of here, sunrise. Buy you breakfast at the club. How about scrambled eggs and a Bloody Mary?"

"Just deliver the money."

"Hey, you're pissed man, I can tell, I get it, he was like your personal driver. Look, I thought I'd bruise him, make it look authentic, all's I'm saying."

"It was authentic all right."

"How do I know he's going to go flying off into the swamp? I'm sorry man, it was like a miscalculation, all's I'm saying. He swerved right into me. See you at oh-seven-hundred, okay?"

"So you got your gook, didn't you, Skinner?"

"Come on, man, that's harsh."

"Just the cash," I said. "That's all I want from you now."

"Get over it, Peckfogle. He was probably VC anyway."

CHAPTER NINETEEN

I was short money when I met Crocodile on the upstairs porch of the Perfume Club.

There was no grenade screen up there, your first hint that this whorehouse was a VC operation. Any bordello making big money fed the profits to Crocodile's sponsors, the Binh Xuyen, who in turn paid off/spied for the Viet Cong.

Crocodile sat at his lacquered table enjoying a mandarin's breakfast feast: Sticky rice with hot dogs and boiled duck eggs. He looked up from his meal with a warm, engaging smile.

"Speck Focal," he said. "I am honored."

His filthy boonie hat sat near his rice bowl and he pushed it across the table to clear space for me. That hat was adorned with all sorts of patches, the meaning of which I did not understand.

Did they represent his victims?

His stumpy fingers worked chopsticks, and he ate greedily, almost as if I wasn't there. His bad eye, usually pearl white, had turned a vile, jaundiced yellow.

"I'm a little short," I said.

He gave me a long, long look with his good eye. "You lie."

"Not much," I said.

"You would not dare."

I began to tremble, I was sure he noticed, a flush passed through me and I touched the chair-back so I would not fall.

"You have one hour."

"I'm five hundred short, that's all. Surely you can come up with ..."

"Sit."

I obeyed.

"I will teach you a lesson, Speck Focal, you are an amateur at this game." He pushed away his rice bowl, drummed the table with his damaged fingers. "You have the money?"

"In my cargo pockets."

"Then we go."

Crocodile left me sitting there worrying for four or five minutes while he attended some business in a back room of the club. He reappeared carrying an attaché case as if he were a Swiss banker. His stunted fingers could not grip the handle, so he carried it between arm and ribcage and then lowered it to the table.

In that case were rolls of US cash, and I added my $5000, which Crocodile counted and bundled in rubber bands. Then he snapped the briefcase shut and led me down the stairs.

"You are one thousand short," he grumbled. "Patience fee, remember?"

"You are going to make a fortune on this deal, okay?"

"Business," he said, and waved and cooed for a rickshaw taxi. "All business is genius, Peckfogle. Have you stopped to consider? We are monkeys come down from the trees, and why? The monkey was happy atop the tree, but he climbed down to do business. Greed brought him down to earth."

He patted the briefcase as the rickshaw drove up, its motorcycle driven by a woman. I had seen her plenty around Cong Ly Street, most recently guarding the gold merchant's shop. She was huge, for a Vietnamese, well fed, with a severe face, and was dressed in dark but clean rags. Those loose rags likely concealed some sort of automatic weapon.

She was a VC operative. Or Binh Xuyen thug, hard to tell the difference, and anyway, the loyalties here were ever-shifting.

I sat beside Crocodile and wondered if this was my Appointment in Samara. If so, I was oddly at peace with it. Du Ky's murder demanded revenge, and if the gods chose me, what the hell. I was defenseless if Crocodile meant to steal my $5000 and leave me in a ditch. In a way, being murdered would be the easy way out, although my Inner Coward was already requesting that it be painless.

We were driven through choking, halting traffic in a city that had grown more prosperous, dangerous and chaotic as the war dragged on. The husky silent woman proved a prudent driver, her black rags flapping in the breeze. The traffic loosened when we veered toward the port and rode into a dense river fog. At a guard shack beside a filthy rusty Chinese cargo ship, the driver glided to a halt.

Crocodile led me up the rusty grimy gangplank while the driver stood grim on the dock.

On the main deck, down a dark passage, we thumped over steel floors and into a cramped, dark stateroom.

It had no portholes, all its white paint was peeling, and it seemed to be used mostly for smoking and playing cards.

Sitting behind a steel table were two uniformed Arvin officers who spoke no English, at least not to me. The tall, fat one glared at me, eyes shining in hate. The single star on his epaulets, if genuine, marked him as a Brigadier General.

His companion, short and skinny with a brush haircut and no obvious rank, walked around from behind the table and offered Salem cigarettes and we all lit up. They spoke Vietnamese in a way that sounded nervous.

Crocodile lay the briefcase on that steel desk.

Neither the general nor his flunky put a hand on it.

His good eye flashing at me, Crocodile spoke in Vietnamese, and I had the distinct feeling he was showing me off. *Look, gentlemen, I bring you exhibit A, my pet American, you see how easy it is to corrupt these fools? Don't worry, this one does as I say.*

The General blew a huge cloud of smoke and Crocodile scolded me: "Stand straight. Do not slouch. You are being judged."

I hadn't realized I was slouching. I recalled Sister Charles patrolling the classroom, tapping our desks with her pointer, and screeching: "Posture!"

The General inclined his head toward me and said something that made Crocodile and the Flunky laugh.

Crocodile said: "They want to know if you like *Get Smart.*"

"What?"

"On your American television. The spy who talks into his shoe."

"Ah..."

"It is the General's favorite show."

A horn honked down on the dock and the General smiled and gave Crocodile a subtle nod. Crocodile turned and led me out into the fog, down the shaky gangplank to the dock. His driver had swapped rickshaw for gun jeep, American made, but with ARVN markings. Crocodile rode shotgun. I climbed into the back beside a duffel bag.

I patted it. Dope, I assumed, worth more than $100,000 at retail. In this impoverished nation, that sum would make you a wealthy man. Above my head was fixed a 60-caliber machinegun with trailing brass ammo belt. We were not going to be robbed without a firefight.

Back we drove, out of the river fog and into the wet heat, to the Perfume Club. I followed Crocodile up the stairs, lugging the duffel bag. The driver, who had not said a word since she appeared, stationed herself in the stairway, scanning the street below. I heaved the duffel bag atop the bar, and opened its top, peered in, laughed, and zipped it shut.

Crocodile held out his stumpy fingers for a shake, American style.

"Two Gentlemen from Verona," he said.

"You ..."

"Shakespeare. Two gentlemen set off on an adventure, but one is in love, and that is his fall down."

"I didn't know you were a..."

"Oh, we are cultured. What do you see when you look at a Vietnamese, Speck Focal? Ignorance? Poverty? Shame? Degradation? We were cultured for a thousand years by the time Columbus scalped his first Indian."

He led me into a dark back room where a wide steel locker had been left open. I heaved the duffel bag in, and Crocodile closed the heavy door, and secured it with a combination lock.

"It will be safe," he said. "Thuy will see to that."

Finally I knew her name. Thuy, the grim-faced driver, had eased into the room, and I looked up to see her, scowling and black-robed.

Like a lethal Sister Charles.

I burst into the STEAM BATH MASSAGE to find Merci's desk abandoned, so I climbed the stairs but she wasn't there either, and the apartment was a mess: bed a riot of rumpled sheets and dishes piled in the tub sink and lousy with roaches.

That wasn't the way Merci kept house.

Back at the STEAM BATH MASSAGE I pushed through the foggy glass door and shouted for her but then saw she was taking a steam.

Naked against white tiles.

There was a whole row of GI uniforms hung on wood pegs and my uniform went up there too and when I was naked I slipped into the hot wet white little room.

"You!" said Merci, and flashed me a look and then stared down at her red-painted toes.

"Why are you mad?" I said.

"Shit head."

"Who?"

"You."

"I'm trying to..."

She turned away, arms wrapped around her as if shielding her breasts from an ogling stranger.

"Where's Du Ky?" she demanded.

"Dead."

"And how?"

"I don't know."

"Fucking liar. Best friends! "

"Merci..."

"We are real people, you know. Not shit-brains like you say. Not gooks. We live and die and cry, like you."

"It was an accident," I lied.

I hate you, John Jay Peckfogle.

Did I say that, or merely think it?

"A GI killed him," I said. "Yes that's true."

"I know so."

"How do you know?"

"Everybody says. Dropped him from the helicopter. People see! I know your GI tricks."

"No."

"You lie like shit."

"A GI killed him," I admitted.

"Say again?"

"A GI smashed his cyclo."

"Likely story."

"That GI is going to prison."

She worked her feet into white flip-flops and jiggled them. "Never happen, GI."

That was the moment when I understood how Merci saw me.

I was a GI.

Just another GI, now.

Way too many bad things had happened to this woman for her to trust anyone, let alone me, member of the invasive species.

With three words, Merci had put me in my place, punctured my romantic dream, and made me realize we had no future.

She was a misfit Vietnamese, and I was a misfit American.

But misfit was all we had in common.

Even her experience with the Catholic church was radically different, in a harsh orphanage that made Saint Sebastian High School seem like Princeton Prep.

I was enraged by Du Ky's murder, but I didn't expect her to ever believe that.

I stood up from the tile bench, kissed the top of her steam-damp hair and said, "That GI is going to prison. You'll see."

I stepped out of the steam room, and took a cold shower.

Alone.

So the locals believed that GIs took Du Ky for a helicopter ride, tortured him for information, and then threw him to his death in the swamp. Multiply that suspicion by a million and it's no wonder GIs were murdered daily on the streets.

I waited out the afternoon in the second-floor safety of VC headquarters, aka The Perfume Club. Merci's revolver was like a lead weight in my cargo pocket.

There were six prostitutes on duty and I bought each one a $5 "champagne," aka Coke thinned with water. It was like making a small donation to the VC, but my mind was too foggy, too busy, for fine distinctions. I asked the girls, in return for my patronage, if they would let me sit at the corner table, unbothered.

At the far table, I could peer over the red-painted balcony rail and watch the streets. I fetched a pack of worn-out playing cards and laid out game after game of Solitaire.

Even when I won there was nothing to win.

Behind me, the girls watched Viet soap operas and gabbed.

Crocodile passed once on his yellow Honda, but didn't look up.

I had the feeling I was looking down from a pacified Heaven on this enormous smoggy beehive of a city, buzzing with pointless activity.

Where do all you people think you're going?

At last, Skinner pulled up in his jeep and parked across the street from the Marilyn Monroe. I watched like a man in a trance as he hustled across the street and into the café.

My hour had come.

Let him worry, I told myself, let him fret a while.

I got high on The Blend and my brain got lazy and I just sat there dreamy, watching, the dope had transformed my attitude, what a beautiful city this was, all these hustlers beneath me now, and I watched entranced until Skinner gave up. Leaving his jeep parked, he whistled for a rickshaw at the doorway of the Marilyn Monroe.

I figured Skinner was headed back to base to fulfill his part in the conspiracy. Stoned, I no longer cared if The Main Deal worked or not.

"See you in hell, Skinner," I muttered and arose, ducked into the back room, opened the combination lock, hefted the duffel bag out of the locker, dragged it across the floor and bumped it down the stairs.

Didn't matter if I damaged the merchandise.

Didn't matter at all.

I slammed the big green bag into the back of Skinner's jeep and drove it to the traffic circle and then along so-called Freedom Road.

I pulled off to the mud shoulder and idled while behind me the sun slanted toward the palmy horizon.

Just at sundown I lurched back into traffic and got in line for the Main Gate, behind two deuce-and-a-halfs and a jeep. MPs and their canine counterparts were inspecting the cargo bay of one of the trucks, canvas flung open.

An ambulance roared up behind me, no siren, just idled, engine loud and out of tune.

As the dogs and MPs jumped down from the truck in front of me, a burst of machine gun fire broke out near Skinner's tower.

It was just like we planned it.

The MPs looked at one another and shouted at their buddies in the sandbagged guard shack.

Pop pop pop, just rifle fire now.

Then a boom, grenade or Claymore, hard to tell.

Then the whole perimeter on the swamp side of the base seemed to open up at once, volleys of fire, coming in waves. The assault siren wailed. Just as the gloom of night edged in on us, the MPs swung open the gate and waved us all in.

I sped along the muddy road to Graves Registration while all around me, GIs, weapons in hand, were sprinting for the defenses at the perimeter. Armored tracks pulled out of the motor pool and skidded around corners. Lights flashed up and down the wire and the first chopper lifted off from in front of the maintenance shed.

There were only two guys on this base who knew this wasn't a real assault. One of them, me, parked the jeep behind Graves Registration at the stacks of empty coffins.

I heaved the duffel bag into a coffin.

An ambulance roared down the mud road and jerked to a stop at the ammo dump and men jumped out. Three of them ran for the parked helicopters on the flight line and two ran into the ammo dump.

All of them wore black pajamas.

I knew I was seeing VC fighters but my dope-addled brain could not react to it. The VC in the ammo dump scurried back to the ambulance and it careened behind a helicopter's blast wall, and then I was blinded by a flash of the purest, whitest light I had ever seen.

Then a shockwave moved like an earthquake through the air. The force of it knocked me over.

I landed flat on my back and a long time later, it seemed, a crack of intense thunder rolled over the sky like a dry ocean wave. This was accompanied by a mechanical sound, like the clattering of a thousand manual typewriters.

I could only see a rectangle of sky and realized I had fallen into a coffin, my duffel bag of dope half-crushed underneath me.

The sounds of somebody else's war seemed real, but far, far distant as I lay in that coffin, safe as death. *John Jay Peckfogle*, a voice seemed to say, *stay right where you are.* Something rumbled by me, something on tracks, maybe a tank or troop carrier. I heard the unmistakable whining of helicopter gunships warming up.

Now there were only two guys on this base who knew that a fake assault had turned real.

Through passing wisps of gun smoke I could see the stars of Heaven. This vision was obliterated by another flash, another rumble of the earth, and I realized the ammo dump was cooking off, and might be exploding all night. I squiggled and writhed in my narrow coffin-bunker and unzipped the duffel bag and rearranged the cartons so that they were insulation between me and all danger. I reserved a few cartons for a pillow. I drew Merci's pistol from my cargo pocket and rested it on my belly. Above me, a Cobra gunship dove at the perimeter, unleashing a red flow of tracers that looked like a river of glowing paint flowing from sky to ground. Flash, flash, the gunship let off two rockets and then U-turned toward the stars.

I lit a Blend cigarette.

I inhaled.

Oh Lord, I prayed, make me unreal.

And then I fell.

Asleep.

I dreamed I was in a coffin-boat, paddling toward New Jersey across a dark and tossing sea.

Merci was drowning in that sea.

Maybe it was the first glint of sunshine that woke me up. Or maybe it was the notes of reveille playing over the loudspeakers. Or maybe it was the rumbling hunger that always followed a Blend high.

But I awoke dry-mouthed and bleary in that coffin, surrounded by a fortune in half-crushed opium cigarettes.

Clutching Merci's pistol in one hand, I lifted myself up for a peek.

The coffins around me were dotted and flecked with shrapnel, BBs and flechette arrows. A huge pall of black smoke hung over what used to be the ammo dump. A wrecked scorched Huey helicopter lay on its side at the end of the flight line, and when I looked past that, I saw three other wrecked choppers, burnt black inside their revetments.

It was already beastly hot and a line of shirtless GIs were combing the main road, in suspicion that VC sappers had planted land mines.

Stiff and sore I arose from the coffin and pocketed the revolver. I covered that dope-filled coffin, and heaved three empty coffins crosswise atop it. I dragged six other coffins in front of that, as stumbling blocks, hoping the morticians would choose these first. I had no idea how many GIs had been killed overnight.

I staggered through the sandbag maze and into my dark dank room and found one tiny envelope of powdered coffee in my footlocker. I switched on the company radio, which was all static, and then Armed Forces Radio Saigon, which was playing *Raindrops Keep Falling on My Head*.

Certainly if we'd had a huge number of men killed, or if the assault on our base had been part of an NVA attack on Saigon, the radio would be all bulletins.

Comforted in the knowledge that last night had been less than a total disaster, I took from a desk drawer a hunk of C-4 explosive, fuel to heat my coffee. I grabbed my steel mess-kit coffee cup and brought it out to the shower room to fill it with water.

As soon as I walked in I realized how badly I needed a wash up, and so I shed my skanky uniform, stood under cool water, and scrubbed up with a stray bar of Ivory soap.

The soggy wooden door creaked open and Miss Hahn peeked in.

"Mời vào," I said.

She slipped in, hunched and sneaky.

It was too early for hooch maids to be on the base.

The morning after an attack, the MPs would be slow and methodical letting Viet workers through the gate, if they let any in at all.

Miss Hanh, hmmm.

Did she have a secret lover in Graves Registration?

Had she hidden on base overnight?

Or ...

"Chào buổi sang," she said with a nervous smile.

"Good morning to you."

I turned my back on her and rinsed off.

And then I had the hunch that turning my back on her wasn't such a good idea.

So I spun around.

But Miss Hanh was sitting demurely on a wooden bench, staring down as if something very interesting was written into the concrete floor. Her conical hat was in her lap, and she kept fidgeting with it.

I had no towel so when I sat dripping on the bench beside her, I played Mister Modesty and draped my fatigue shirt over my lap.

"You're early," I said.

She looked at me wide, eyed, fear.

"Earl-lee," I said. "You. Time."

"No bic."

She wore a purple blouse, black trousers, cheap flip-flops, conical hat with purple ribbon, I had never seen her in anything else. But now I noticed a watch.

A gold watch.

Which I had never seen before.

A watch is nothing in America, but in Vietnam, it's a symbol of wealth.

Wealthy 19-year-old laundress.

Peckfogle, you fool.

Staring into her upturned hat, she, suddenly fluent, said: "Mister Sang asked me to speak with you."

I leaned forward, elbows on naked knees, staring at the wet floor.

"Mister Sang?" I muttered.

"Yes."

"Mister Sang from Cong Ly Street?"

"That is the one."

"You are at work very early this morning, no?"

"Yes."

"So you do understand *early*."

"Yes."

"You understand English very well."

"Perhaps."

"You hid on the base last night."

"Mister Sang ..."

"Known on the street as Crocodile."

"So the GIs call him."

"Crocodile said I would have something for you?"

"Yes."

"A delivery."

"Yes."

"What happens after I deliver to you?"

"I don't know. It is a very large bag. I need it please."

"Let me..."

She stood and put on her hat.

"Now or never," she said, her tone harsh, her eyes hard. "No wasting time, no fooling."

"Follow me," I said.

So she's a genuine VC operative, I mused, as I led the tricky laundress away from the shower room. Or maybe a stooge for the Binh Xuyen gang. You never know over here.

Ignoramus.

She followed me, pulling her rickety home-built wagon, in which was stuffed a duffel bag full of laundry. She clomped behind me along the boardwalk, across a steel plank over a ditch, and then into the coffin yard behind Graves Registration.

With help from this wily spy I worked my way back through the coffins and uncovered the stash of *Le Rêve*. I stuffed the cartons into the duffel bag, keeping two for myself.

Miss Hanh stood, hands on hips. "All of them, please."

"These are mine."

She shook her head. "Can't help it, GI. You will be in big trouble."

I zipped the duffel bag. "Here. Go. Before I call the MPs."

"You don't dare."

"Watch me."

She spit, not at me, but off to the side. "You will pay."

"Go!"

I loaded the duffel bag into her wagon. The decoy duffel bag, full of laundry, she flipped into the mud. Without a word or a glance, she tugged that wagon out of the coffin yard.

I ran my two cartons into my bunker, slammed them into my footlocker, and then dashed to tail Miss Hanh, a sneaky block behind. She walked without looking back to the concession laundry, a Viet-run business that occupied a seedy muddy building near the motor pool.

I retreated to my bunker, stuffed my two cartons into a rucksack, and marched toward Skinner's barracks. I didn't get that far, because Skinner stood, head down as if in contemplation, in the long breakfast line outside the mess hall.

He perked up when he saw me.

"Dibs on your bacon," he said.

"Sure," I said.

"Life ain't fakin' when you've got bacon. What you got there?"

I turned to give him a full view of the rucksack. "It's for you."

"The fuck?"

He looked around paranoid, as if the MPs were closing in. He stepped out of line, and tugged me by the shirtsleeve, and we walked off to stand in the shadow of the mess hall's wooden water tower.

"I brought your share," I said.

"My share?"

"The payoff is in product."

"Fuck-O-Rama! You've got it strapped to your back?"

"Well, I can't send 'em special delivery, can I?"

"This was a cash deal!"

"Skinner, this is two grand, wholesale, so you already got your money back, and there's more to come."

"Aw, Peckfogle, you fuck-up, you major league fuck-up. I knew I couldn't count on you."

"Just take it and enjoy the ride, Skinner. You'll be a big man on base for a long, long time."

I set the rucksack at his feet. "Take it away. It's yours now. Our deal is done, and we're no longer friends."

I glanced at the long line of hungry soldiers, none of whom was paying particular attention to us.

Skinner said: "We're not finished, Peckfogle, you and me."

CHAPTER TWENTY

In Colonel Sadler's office, I discovered my inner Leading Man. My Big Scene had arrived. I was ready for my close-up.

Literally a close-up. Warrant Officer Brennan topped a tripod with a movie camera and pointed the lens at me.

I sat up straight as a Catholic schoolboy, facing Colonel Sadler office across his no-nonsense desk. On it was a plain green blotter, a clean glass ashtray, and a tiny silver cross set upon a silver Hill of Calvary.

Behind him was a row of stand-up flags, like he was an ambassador for the United Nations. Photographs of his glory days reminded visitors that, among other triumphs, he had crowded into the White House Rose Garden with a stiff group of his peers and Vice President Spiro Agnew.

Brennan set the camera whirring and clicking, and then stood behind my chair so that I couldn't see him. My ears rang with an unfamiliar hum.

Air conditioning.

From my pocket I extracted a pack of *Le Rêve*, and, trying to play it casual, spun it on the Colonel's desk.

This was improv. Nobody had written a script.

"Manufactured in the tribal jungles of Laos by the Binh Xuyen," I said.

The Colonel cut me off. "We're interested in your direct knowledge. Leave the theories to us."

Chastened, I described to the Colonel and the camera the Arvin General and his Flunky aboard the Chinese cargo ship at Pier 12 on the Saigon River. The silent scary female goon Thuy dressed in black rags. The Arvin gun jeep with M-60, draped in brass ammo. The VC offices in the back rooms of the Perfume Club.

"How do you know it's VC?" Brennan grumbled behind me.

"I've been back there, it's Crocodile's office." I turned to squint at Brennan. "You know Crocodile?"

"We know Crocodile."

"Miss Hanh, the laundress at Graves Registration, she's his agent on base, and the big stash is over at the post laundry right now. Crocodile, he is VC, right?"

Brennan shrugged.

"It's best not to make assumptions," the Colonel said. "We find ourselves in a complex situation here. There's a lot of loyalty overlap."

"A hell of an overlap," Brennan said.

The MP radio behind him squawked with static and mumbled curses.

"Can I ask you guys something?"

"You can ask," Brennan said.

I swiveled in my chair, looking from him to the Colonel.

"There was a schoolgirl, Sanny, that's not her Vietnamese name, but it's the only name I know her by. She was a waitress, injured in a fragging downtown. They treated her here for two days and then flew her off to Japan."

That roused no reaction from either lifer.

"Doesn't that seem ..." I waggled my hand "... was she working for us? You guys wouldn't use a schoolgirl, would you?"

"We should focus ..." said the Colonel.

"... on the drug transaction," Brennan finished for him.

If the CID had used Sanny as an informer, then they knew about me, my drug habits, about Merci, about my daily bribes at the Main Gate.

"This man you met on the ship, whom you call the General," Brennan said. "Describe him for us."

I went through it all, maybe for twenty minutes, every detail I could think of. I dared not lie or fudge. They probably already knew some of what I had to tell them. At the last stop on the Rat Express, I threw Skinner off the train.

"Two cartons," I said. "At his hooch right now. And it was his money that financed the deal."

"Where'd he get the money?" Brennan asked.

"From his mother, some of it. And some of it, he stole by ripping off the mail."

"The mail?"

"The cash that GIs send home. He did a one-day rip, or so he told me."

The Colonel stared me down and said: "This is Skinner, the postal clerk, the one with the shaving profile?"

"Yes," I said, my lips moving, my heart shut cold.

"You realize," the Colonel said, "you may be asked to testify. Could you do that in open court?"

Remembering Du Ky, dead in the swamp with a broken neck, I said: "Yes, Sir. Yes, Sir, I'll stand before a judge."

I was feeling shaky as I walked from the Colonel's office to the Main Gate.

I wasn't used to siding with Authority.

It rattled me.

I figured Skinner wouldn't make it to sundown. They didn't need a warrant to search his hooch.

No matter that Skinner had killed my friend Du Ky, LBJ is a terrible fate, and nobody deserves to be locked in a shipping cage, set out in such fierce heat, with no human contact except for the sadistic guards.

Not even Skinner deserved that.

I had avenged Du Ky, but I didn't feel good about it at all.

I was relieved that so far Brennan and the Colonel had not asked me to reveal the names of the buyers of those first two cartons. Apparently the Colonel wanted to make just one big splashy arrest, and turn Skinner into an example.

In that way, the Colonel was like Sister Charles' hero, Saint Charles Borromeo.

Who burned witches at the stake.

As an example.

To keep everybody else in line.

I stopped a block short of Main Gate and, on hands and knees, puked in a ditch. That left me with such a lousy taste in my mouth that I detoured to the Newbie Barracks to buy a "Pepsi" from SSG Foster.

"You're lucky," I told the old sarge.

"You're shitting me," he said, and poured Southern Comfort into his Bakelite coffee mug. His bleary eyes clouded over when he said, "Horse shit duty like this? Do I look lucky to you?"

"Very," I said.

"How so?"

"You'll never know."

"What the goddang hell you talking about?"

"Somebody's watching over you, Foster."

"Shit you say."

"Maybe there is a God after all."

"That's twenty five cents for the Pepsi."

"These are on you," I said, and fetched another can from the tub before I walked away.

At Main Gate I laid a can of lukewarm 7-Up on the dirty plywood counter and said: "Rough night?"

"No assholes out, no assholes in," grunted Freckles the MP. Gone was the friendly, aw-shucks grin. These Main Gate boys hadn't slept for a while.

I said, "You know me, Connors, I'm almost a civilian, counting the hours, that's how short I am."

"No assholes out," he said. "No assholes in."

"But I'm not an asshole, you know that. Come on. I'm so short I could sit on a doughnut and swing my legs."

"Two guys KIA last night," he said, "chopper crash".

"It's war, man, it does happen, with sappers running around. Ammo dump? We're lucky it wasn't a lot worse."

"Back off, Peckfogle, or I'm gotta shoot you."

Fuck you, Freckles the MP.

Asshole.

This base would collapse into the mud without its Viet employees, but for today, they were all sent home when they reported to the gate. The one exception was Mr. Phan. War, peace, plague or famine, unless it was the End Times, the honey wagon had to clean out those latrines.

So I waited at the EM Club, shooting billiards against whatever loafer would play me, steadily losing $1 a game, ordering French Fries for breakfast and lunch, until finally I saw Mr. Phan's honey wagon at its last stop behind the PX.

I hitched a $20 ride out with him, ducking to the floorboards as we passed Main Gate. I insisted on a ride all the way down to the Avenue of Whores. The stinking truck let me off just in front of the Hollie Wood Theater, which had re-strung the banner that said: LOVE STORY with RYAN O'NEAL.

It was a forlorn sight, Cong Ly Street without its GIs. This city had become addicted to the dollar bill, and now its cafes were quiet, its bars dark, its bordellos ripe with restless, sulking unemployed girls, fearing, I supposed, a return to the rice paddies.

I found Crocodile sitting on his motorcycle in a dank alley behind the Perfume Club.

"Okay, I delivered. We're good, right?"

"For now," he said. "You don't expect cash, I hope."

He turned his blind eye toward me.

"Oh yes I do expect cash," I said. "American cash."

"You were two cartons short," he said.

"That's Skinner's take. I want mine in cash."

He laughed. "I am testing you. I'm glad you did not get angry. It shows good judgment."

"I just need the money now."

"Okay. No hard feelings, partner, as your John Wayne says."

He tooted his motorcycle horn twice. Down the Perfume Club's dark back stairs strode Thuy, his female bodyguard in black rags.

Crocodile whispered and she retreated. He asked me: "So what will you do with your money?"

"Maybe you can help there. I need a visa issued to Merci, and I can pay up to a thousand bucks."

Crocodile laughed. "Passports are twenty thousand these days."

"She already has a passport."

"Under what name?"

"Merci Negroni."

Crocodile shook his head. "I do not think so."

"What do you mean?"

"I have that passport."

"What are you talking about?"

"I have all the passports of all the whores on my street."

"She is not a whore."

I stepped back. I needed to think for a moment, and to keep myself from taking a swing at Crocodile. "How much for her passport?"

"For you?" He offered me a Kool. "Discount. Your profit plus $10,000."

I reached for the cigarette, and it snapped in half.

"Fair?" he said.

I looked over my shoulder as Thuy crept up behind me. She offered Crocodile a folded, dirty manila envelope, but he indicated with a tilt of his head that she should hand it to me.

"Before I'd pay, I'd want to see the passport," I said. "I want to see it's valid."

Thuy turned and mounted the stairs.

"Five thousand," I said. "That's all I'll pay. I need her passport and visa, both."

"Visa to where?"

"United States."

He laughed. "I don't think so. Very expensive, America. Everyone wants to go there these days."

"Thailand."

"Maybe for ten thousand altogether. It is not simple, Speck Focal. There are bribes to pay."

"It's her passport, come on."

"And it's my country, but here you are, pissing and shitting on it every day. Do you have a license, Speck Focal, to shit on my country?"

He looked me up and down as if he'd never seen me before. "You smell of something, what I cannot quite say. Your whore owns a steam bath, so perhaps you should clean up."

"We're partners, remember? I want her passport."

"I know you GIs. I know your evil natures, you cannot fool a Crocodile. Very shrewd animals."

I lit a stub of that broken Kool. Its menthol tasted unspeakably vile. Which meant it was knock-off version of The Blend.

"You were short," Crocodile said.

"That was Skinner's cut."

"Oh, I see! Now Speck Focal makes the decisions. Perhaps you think you can run my business, Speck Focal."

Thuy descended the stairs, walked around the motorcycle and handed a green passport book to Crocodile. He did not examine it, but tucked it into his fatigue shirt pocket.

"Trust," he said. "Nine thousand, final price for your whore's exit papers. You can never call Crocodile a stubborn man."

I crushed the cigarette under the sole of my combat boot.

"Come on," he said, "you GIs, you're made of money."

I had a flash of insight then.

Merci.

Here was a woman who had survived a hungry childhood.

She was a rice hoarder.

She had at least one hidden gun.

She was an obsessive bookkeeper.

Which meant she had money stashed somewhere.

I walked away from Crocodile and out into the fading afternoon sunshine of Cong Ly Street, confident that I could work a deal. Even if all Merci had stashed was a couple of grand, I might be able to knock Crocodile down to $7,000 or so.

I already had $5,000 in a wrinkled envelope in my cargo pockets. Yes, I had counted it. American $20s and $50s. You'd better believe I counted it.

But Merci wasn't at her desk. Nor was she upstairs in the apartment. I took a Blend break on the balcony, watching the street through the grenade screen. With a flick of the finger, I dislodged chunks of glass shrapnel.

On the other side of that screen I saw not the dirty chaotic city, but what I imagined: a vision of my saintly glory as I, the best Son a Mother ever had, freed my mom from a Mormon prison. This triumph was followed instantly by my magical transportation to Bayway, where Miss Malecki, tears dripping from her angel-blue eyes, confessed that she had always loved me.

The Blend.

A miracle in every puff.

My dream bubble burst when I saw Merci hop out of a rickshaw.

That was real.

She dodged across the street but there was something strange about her, I couldn't figure it. I heard her downstairs, unlocking the steel door. She mounted the stairs and appeared in the doorway. I said hello vaguely but my eyes focused on her right hand.

Which was bandaged.

So clean and white it might have been done at the headquarters of Johnson & Johnson.

"Merci," I said.

She slipped that bandaged hand behind her.

"What happened to you?" I asked.

"Does not matter," she said.

"What do you mean it doesn't matter?"

"I am going to Nepal."

"What do you mean going to Nepal?"

"Can't you hear?"

"Talk to me."

"I will pay a smuggler."

"With what money?"

"Never mind."

"Smuggler? They'll take your money and laugh. Or kill you and dump you in the jungle."

"Don't care."

"Well, I do. I have money for you. But not to pay a smuggler."

I grabbed her wrist and gawked at her bandage.

"What happened to your hand?"

"Shut up."

Three fingers she could wiggle. Everything else from knuckles to wrist was wrapped in white. But most of her pinky was missing.

"Who did this to you?"

"Sister Helena."

I took me a moment to regroup. "No, not who bandaged you, who hurt you?"

She yanked her hand out of my grasp. "Nobody. It's how you GIs say. Just say fuck it and drive on."

"Crocodile," I muttered.

I sat at our bare wood kitchen table, set for soup for two, and put my head in my hands. Merci, only her left hand free, unbuttoned her blouse and turned the black Westinghouse fan toward her sweaty chest.

"Next life," she said, "I will be a child's doctor in Nepal. Taking care of orphan babies."

I sat stupid at the table, trying to absorb what was plainly the truth. "Crocodile cut you."

"We all suffer this war, now it is my turn."

"He cut your finger off."

She reached into her ragged cloth purse and brought out a tiny white bottle. "I have pills. From the good sister."

"He cut your fucking finger off."

I rose from the table and walked out on the balcony and then spun around and called in: "I was short money, so he cut your fucking finger off."

"It is not a big deal, Jay. He has done this to other girls. We must accept there is a price. He is a big-time shit-face gangster. My hand will heal. It is his way. You can do nothing."

"Fuck that," I said.

The sun went down in a tropical flash, winked out like a bum light bulb.

I dug into the rice vase and pulled out Merci's shiny little revolver. I used a camouflage t-shirt to wipe it free of rice talc.

She gave me a horrified look and her lips trembled.

"I'll be back," I said.

I rushed out of there before she could say a word. I unlocked the steel door and pushed out onto the street, my way blocked by a small crowd under the banner LOVE STORY with RYAN O'NEAL

I realized I was holding a pistol and dropped it into my trouser pocket. Nobody in the theater line even seemed to notice.

I walked around the clump of movie patrons, all of them Vietnamese, and my legs carried me, without really engaging my will, to the corner where I could hear Crocodile's motorcycle idling.

I could smell its exhaust.

And the moldering trash smell of that alley.

I paused at the corner.

I imagined Crocodile chopping Merci's finger off, envisioned it happening at her desk, blood spurt, scream, the massage girls running for the exits.

Of course he would do it for an audience. Humiliation and power, that was the point.

I rounded the corner.

"Peckfogle, my friend," he said.

Then he grinned in gold.

"Oh," he said. "You cannot be as angry as you look. You are so red in the face, you'll have a stroke, I fear. You were warned. You were told not to cheat me."

I looked over his head to the Perfume Club entrance.

Woman goon not in sight.

I grasped that revolver, lifted it out of my pocket and pointed it at Crocodile.

His face set hard.

His eyes cold like a snake's.

"You cannot..."

The gun went off.

I do not remember pulling the trigger.

But Crocodile flew backward.

I was spattered with tissue, blood and fragments of gold.

He landed on his side in the filthy alley behind his motorcycle and flopped over onto his belly and did a low crawl for maybe three or four yards, leaving a blood trail and then with a great shudder and anguished cry, his soul left his body.

He collapsed into nothing but tissue and bone.

I leaned over him, rolled him over, ripped Merci's passport out of his top pocket.

His mouth was a bloody ugly hole, his eyes open in final surprise.

His expression seemed to say: Peckfogle, we were such good friends.

I looked up and there at the balcony of the Perfume Club stood Thuy the female goon.

Watching.

Stone faced.

Making no move at all.

I ran away.

I paid twenty five cents admission to LOVE STORY and sat there in the back row, near a giant whirling fan that obliterated all dialog. I needed to calm down in the fantasy darkness.

The movie generated subtitles in French and Vietnamese. As I sat there hyperventilating and shaking ,these words flashed on the screen: *L'amour est ne jamais avoir à dire que vous êtes désolé.*

I left Merci's pistol under the seat and walked out.

CHAPTER TWENTY ONE

A few days later I arrived in California. The long flight gave me time to ponder my transformation from peacenik soldier to cold-blooded killer to rattled civilian.

I distracted myself on that flight by thinking that I would get my mom out of jail. That would turn me into what I'd always wanted to be: a Hero.

How I would free Mom without cash was a problem I put off contemplating. I just wanted to see her and find that she was okay.

The Army's mustering-out pay barely covered my airline ticket from Oakland to Boise, and in Pocatello I discovered I was a day late and a few thousand dollars short. My sister Dolly had bailed Mom out, and they had flown to Dolly's home in Juneau. I called Dolly's roommate, collect, but they hadn't yet arrived.

I needed a Red Cross loan for the air fare back to the East Coast. And it's true, Your Honor, that I got home just in time for Miss Malecki's wedding, with the mud of Vietnam still clinging to my boots.

She's not known as Miss Malecki now.

Obviously.

She lives in New Brunswick, having married an up-and-coming pharmaceuticals salesman at Johnson & Johnson.

I wish the happy couple well.

I did not mean to embarrass her nor disrupt her wedding reception.

Which was a very nice affair, and may I say they put on an excellent spread over at Bayway's Best Banquets, in case you're ever interested.

My mother is back in New Jersey, sir, and I'm living with her for now. Since the divorce, she has reverted to her maiden name, Colleen Mannix. I've been informed by my attorney, and I thank the county for her services, I've been informed that my living arrangements may have to change, since after the adjudication here today, both my mother and I would be felons.

Technically.

Although I'm not assuming I will be sentenced to probation, Your Honor, its my hope that I can live with Mom until things settle down.

As my attorney has reported, I am a witness for the United States Government in a General Courts Martial case scheduled to be heard this winter at Fort Leavenworth, Kansas.

It involves a felony amount of opioid substance, and I was an active government informer whose contribution was vital to that case, as you will see in my file.

In there are commendations from Military Police Commander Colonel William Sadler, and from his investigator, Thomas Brennan.

I have been honorably discharged, and have enrolled under the GI Bill at Bayway Junior College. I am beginning, sir, with courses in American History and Remedial Writing. My English Professor believes medication may cure my compulsion to write in childish one-sentence paragraphs, which he abhors almost as much as my tendency to be overly generous with Capitalization.

Now about the actual incident, Your Honor, I'm here to tell the truth, hand on the Bible, so help me God.

First can we deal with a few of the falsehoods that have spread through the community about this case?

I no longer drink or take drugs, your honor, although I have not yet conquered the nervous cigarette habit.

It is not true that I arrived on a Harley Davidson motorcycle at Mombo Bill's on the morning of Miss Malecki's wedding. It is not true that I proceeded to get roaring drunk well before noon, nor that I started a fight with a tugboat sailor. That particular establishment, sir, is very popular with tugboat crews even in early morning, and it is very unlikely I would have survived an altercation with a tugboat crew.

Nor is it true that I drove a motorcycle over the Goethals Bridge, while insanely drunk, screaming at motorists and weaving in traffic. That is urban legend, sir, and there is proof in the case file that I sold my Triumph Bonneville almost two years ago, the week before I joined the Army.

While we're correcting the record, sir, may I say that I had absolutely nothing to do with the recent Miami Herald investigation of my father, John Adams Peckfogle, known to the public as Adam Peckfogle.

I understand that the Dade County Prosecutor has taken up the case, which involves charities fraud, allegedly, but I strongly deny sir that I have been in contact with either the Herald's reporters or the state's investigators.

I do admit the following:

That on Saturday, June 5, 1970, I, an uninvited guest, appeared at the wedding reception of Mrs. Constance McCabe, nee Malecki, and her husband Fred.

That I appeared in camouflage clothing, which may have given some guests the impression that they were being threatened by an unhinged Vietnam Veteran.

That while the bride and groom and many guests were dancing, I approached the head table and began a conversation with Miss Lenore Milano, better known under her Holy Orders name of Sister Charles Borromeo.

That said conversation got loud.

Particularly on my part.

I acknowledge that I disparaged said person as a "medieval throwback" and blamed her for sending me to Vietnam.

I apologize for that, Your Honor, but I stand by this, however rude it was: I told Sister Charles that as an education professional, it was her duty to recognize that children who act up in school are being abused at home.

Such children should not be doubly abused by their teachers, I said, and accused her of dereliction of duty and heartless cruelty.

That's all I meant to say, Your Honor. It is not true that I screamed the epithet "rotten bitch" as the groomsmen dragged me away.

However, I do admit that just before they escorted me out, I picked up a cake knife.

Now when I say knife, Your Honor, don't think of a lethal instrument, but one of those flimsy, flexible server-type knives that's capable only of slicing a wedding cake.

That's the instrument I used when I gave Sister Charles a whack across the knuckles.

I see it tagged there on the evidence table.

There was no bleeding, nor did the victim seek medical treatment.

Nor is she in this courtroom today.

My real crime, your honor?

I really should be standing before you because I left a good woman behind in Vietnam.

A woman I loved.

I gave her money to buy her way out.

But I don't know what happened to her.

And I fear the worst.

Terrible things happened to those people, Your Honor. It is difficult for Americans to imagine the terror, the treachery and danger they lived with every day. At least a million good people died during our intervention, Your Honor. Including a great many innocents. A million, in such a small nation.

I took the easy way out of that mess for myself.

The money I gave my girlfriend was supposed to ease my conscience.

Only it hasn't.

And now in my selfish way, I've lost track of her, leaving her in the most dangerous city in the world, from where she has already disappeared, for good or for ill I don't know.

I can only hope that she made it to Nepal.

It's true that I have dismissed my court-appointed attorney so that I may represent myself before you. I mean no disrespect, but I feel capable of presenting my own case.

So now I am ready to receive your judgment. May I salute to show you the tattoo that caused me so much trouble in the Army?

It's just three little letters.

At the distance between us, you can barely see them at all.